D0160295

THE
ONES

DANIEL SWEREN-BECKER

New York

[Imprint]
MAKE YOUR MARK

A part of Macmillan Children's Publishing Group

THE ONES. Copyright © 2016 by Daniel Sweren-Becker. All rights reserved. Printed in the
United States of America by R. R. Donnelley & Sons Company, Harrisonburg, Virginia. For
information, address Imprint, 175 Fifth Avenue, New York, N.Y. 10010.

Library of Congress Cataloging-in-Publication Data

Names: Sweren-Becker, Daniel, author.
Title: The Ones / Daniel Sweren-Becker.
Description: First edition. | New York : Imprint, 2016. | Summary:
"Genetically engineered teenagers called 'The Ones' go to extremes fighting
for their rights as society turns against them"— Provided by publisher.
Identifiers: LCCN 2015042697 (print) | LCCN 2016021397 (ebook) |
ISBN 9781250083142 (hardback) | ISBN 9781250083159 (ebook)
Subjects: | CYAC: Science fiction. | Adventure and adventurers—Fiction. |
Genetic engineering—Fiction. | BISAC: JUVENILE FICTION /
Action & Adventure / General. | JUVENILE FICTION / Science Fiction.
Classification: LCC PZ7.1.S946 One 2016 (print) | LCC PZ7.1.S946 (ebook) |
DDC [Fic]—dc23
LC record available at https://lccn.loc.gov/2015042697

Our books may be purchased in bulk for promotional, educational, or business use. Please
contact your local bookseller or the Macmillan Corporate and Premium Sales Department at
(800) 221-7945 ext. 5442 or by e-mail at MacmillanSpecialMarkets@macmillan.com.

Book design by Erin Fitzsimmons and Natalie C. Sousa

Imprint logo designed by Amanda Spielman

First Edition—2016

1 3 5 7 9 10 8 6 4 2

fiercereads.com

If this book shall be took by hook or by crook, then a thousand-year
curse shall never be shook.

**DEDICATED TO
LA-U AND VOLCANO MAN**

FOR THE GENES,
AND THEN EVERYTHING ELSE—
THANK YOU.

THE
ONES

PROLOGUE

YOU BLINK AWAKE, already terrified. Maybe it was a distant footstep or the sound of keys clicking against each other. You crawl quickly to the corner of your cell and hide in the darkness, hide from whoever is coming down that hallway. It never works, not once in all the weeks you've been here, but you do it anyway. You hope that maybe this time they will leave you alone.

You press yourself into that corner, embracing it, begging the walls to help you, literally whispering into the cinder blocks. You love your cell because it is not the interrogation room. It is cold and hard and dark and teeming with roaches, but nothing bad has ever happened here. If only you never had to leave this cell; that is a compromise you'd be willing to make. Especially right now, with a key pushing into the lock on the door.

A woman stands in the doorway and looks down at you. All it takes is a point from her long, bony finger and you know what to do: Stand up, scurry past her down the hallway, and step into the other room. If you resist, she'll drag you anyway. And you don't even have to look, you can already hear them, smell them, taste them—the two empty bags looped through her belt.

The clear bag is for suffocation. They hold it over your head, and you can see through it as you begin to asphyxiate. Watching them look on passively as you struggle to breathe always makes it worse.

The black bag is for water. You are totally blind as they strap your torso down and pour water over your face—buckets of it, freezing and unending. Eventually, you have no choice but to gasp and inhale the water and drown yourself.

Most days they stop just short of killing you. On other days you pass out and wake up in your cell, your torso bruised from the chest compressions they performed to bring you back to life. And somehow you are thankful as you blink awake on that filthy floor. They could have killed you, but they didn't. They tortured you to the brink of death, but no further. Back in your cell, you are safe again.

Until tomorrow.

Before you know it, a day passes and it is time to do it all over again. Or maybe it isn't even a day, just an hour, or maybe even a minute, for all you can tell. There is no time here, no dawns, no dusks, no clocks, no light. No parents, no friends, no school, no hope. There is just your cell and the room with the bag lady. And every time, before she chooses a bag, she smiles and reminds you of the facts of your new life.

You are a terrorist.

We can do whatever we want to you.

You will die in here.

Unless . . .

Unless you answer their questions. It could all be over if you cooperated. You could sleep in your own bed tonight, if you would just answer these few basic questions.

When is the next attack?

Where is Kai hiding?

Who is helping him?

What is the Ark?

What is the Ark?

What is the Ark?

You barely even know what they are talking about, but you can sense their panic, their fear, their determination. You explain that you don't have any answers. They don't believe you. It doesn't make sense to them.

Why would you help these people?

They are ruining America.

Don't you want to protect your country?

They insist you tell them something. But what little you *do* know—any single scrap that might somehow be useful to them—you protect with every fiber of your being. You store it away, hide it, forget it, deny its existence, and make it impossible to retrieve. That is the only contribution you can make now. And giving up on that would feel worse than the bags.

Today the clear bag comes first. The taut plastic is yanked over your head, and by now you know not to shake too much—that only makes things tighter. You know not to jerk your arms—that cuts your wrists against the handcuffs. You know not to panic—that wastes the air too quickly. So you sit calmly as the bag gets tighter and tighter against your face, your throat starting to burn now, your head beginning to feel light, your heart racing. All you can do is stare through the clear plastic at the bag lady and her colleagues. You know they will take off the bag eventually, but each time they seem to wait longer and longer, as if to set a record. You start to gasp now, and you gasp and you gasp and you gasp, but there is no air left to breathe. Still, you know it's too soon for them to stop; you aren't close to the end.

And right here you take a second to consider the absurdity of the situation, as you sit there dying slowly and painfully while public servants from your own government look on, not lifting a finger or even breaking a law. You try to hold your gaze on these people, to judge them, to implore them, to connect in any way possible, but your vision is gone. And then you reach the end and you gasp at nothing now, realizing there is no point, but your brain makes you do it anyway. You are just a dying body, incapable of any more thoughts or decisions. You are nothing. It's over, and they will either let you die or remove the bag. You fade away before you can find out. This is your life now.

You are a terrorist.

We can do whatever we want to you.

You will die in here.

Unless . . .

Unless nothing. There are some things worth dying for.

CHAPTER 1

Four weeks earlier

THE BREATHING HELPED Cody relax. She ran right down the middle of the street and took huge gulps of air, each breath serving to calm her down. The town was silent, the streets empty, but the quiet actually scared her even more. It reminded her of those eerie moments before an earthquake, when all the birds and insects and animals disappear to somewhere safer. Where do they all go? And how do they even know?

Maybe they all had a mother like Cody's—the type of mom who would, without any warning, sometimes give you a look that sent shivers down your spine. Cody always wondered what was in that look, that weird combination of love and hope mixed with something much darker. She had come to sense that it was guilt. Guilt over the choice her mom had made for her. A choice that, in hindsight, was putting Cody in danger now. Cody didn't see it that way, but it still made her uncomfortable. As they sat together watching their old, boxy television, waiting like everyone else to hear the news, she felt her mom staring at her with that look. So Cody grabbed her tattered sneakers, threw on a faded T-shirt, and slipped out the door. Running was always easier than talking. When she ran, she could breathe.

Outside, Cody loped across her patchy front yard and down her gravel street and opened up her stride as she left her crumbling neighborhood behind. She sliced through barren intersections, ignoring the glow of televisions coming out of every home, her dark green eyes staring straight ahead, her thick burgundy hair streaming behind her. Inside those homes, the whole country was watching now, waiting for the decision. But Cody knew what was coming, could smell it in the wind like the birds did. She knew how the Supreme Court would rule and what that would mean for her. Before it happened, she wanted to find James.

Her legs beat a winding path two miles across town, her usual route now too dangerous to traverse. There were houses she didn't want to run past, people in town she'd rather not see. Flags and signs and graffiti everywhere that she wanted to avoid. If she zigged and zagged at all the right places, she could forget about what the rest of the world thought of her.

When she made it to the stately brick house at the end of Argyle Street, Cody cut across the perfectly manicured lawn and went around to a side window to peer over the square hedges. Sure enough, James and his whole family were huddled in front of the TV in their living room. James sat with his perfect posture, his expression calm under his mop of brown curls, even in the face of what he was watching. Cody knew that if she waited a moment, he would catch her gaze eventually. James was oblivious to a lot of things, but never to her. Not the worst trait for your seventeen-year-old boyfriend.

When James finally looked over, she gave him a flick of the eyes, and a minute later he joined her in the street. Before they could speak, Cody was running, James was rushing to catch up, and they were off, the only things moving as dusk settled on Shasta, California.

To see these two run together was like watching a pair of hawks carve through the air or two dolphins crest a wave. The motion suited them, as if they were born for this exact activity. Their bodies were perfectly proportioned, legs and arms churning in mathematically ideal ratios, their powerful inhales timed with exact symmetry to their powerful exhales. They were both beautiful, and the ground flew by underneath them.

They ran to the edge of the residential neighborhood, then climbed the scraggly foothills on the outskirts of town and entered the thicker pine groves, the trail growing rougher, narrower, and steeper. Their gait remained true, each step agile and soft on the dark, rocky earth.

And then, miles above the town, they emerged into a clearing and finally stopped, catching their breath in the clear, piney air. Below them, the town was still, half-lit in the fading sunlight, and a cold autumn wind blew up from the valley.

"What do you think happens next?" Cody asked, finally breaking their silence.

James never lied, so she knew he'd answer honestly, even if he was worried. She looped an arm behind the small of his back and leaned into his body, trying to find shelter from the wind and everything else.

"I don't know," he said. "But no matter what, we're going to be fine."

She pressed into him tightly and tried to believe it.

≈

On their walk back down the trail, they couldn't resist playing a favorite game: trying to kick a single pebble all the way down the hill without picking it up. Most days the pebble would eventually skitter off a ledge or get lost in a bush, but if they ever got it down safely, Cody would take it home and save it. Nothing like a pile of rocks to make your bedroom look cool. They complemented the rest of the mess on her floor—the various telescopes and scales and old medical junk that she liked to pick out at flea markets. It was all part of what James called Cody's "unique" aesthetic: science-geek chic filtered through a vintage lens. But a stranger seeing her room would probably make her out to be a Wild West snake-oil salesman.

James kicked the stone a few feet ahead, taking care to keep it in the middle of the trail. "You gonna stick around for dinner?" he asked.

"And get trapped in a cross-examination about current events from your parents?"

"My mom saw you loitering outside the window."

"*Loitering?* Yikes, she better hide the good china."

"Her word, not mine. She said that if you won't come in, she's going to put a saucer of milk out for you. I told her a tray of brownies would work a lot better."

"Sounds great."

"Come on, Cody. I know they're kind of intense, but they like you, I promise."

Please, Cody thought. *Do they ask other dinner guests if their coats have bedbugs?*

"It's your brother, too," Cody said. "Every time we're together, he can't help staring daggers at us."

"He does not stare daggers at us."

"Fine, butter knives. But it's still weird."

"It's not easy for him to be the odd man out. When the three of us are together, he's the one who's different."

"No one would even know if he didn't make a big deal about it!" Cody exclaimed. She kicked the stone and took a breath. "And today . . . he's going to be gloating."

"Even more reason why I need you around. Unless, of course, you want me to deal with it all alone," James said, slumping his shoulders in exaggerated rejection.

Cody couldn't help but smile, even as she shook her head. "I hate when you do this."

"Outsmart you to get what I want?" James replied, grinning at her.

"No. I hate when you *think* you've outsmarted me, even though you didn't."

"You're staying for dinner, aren't you?" James gave the stone a powerful kick with his fancy neon running shoe, and it tumbled down into the brush. Cody watched it disappear and then gave him a shove, sending James scurrying down the slope.

"Not cool! I liked that one."

James let his momentum take him down the hill. "Come on," he yelled. "We're late."

=

Without any time to go home, Cody had to shower in James's bathroom, but she still took as long as possible to delay going downstairs. Plus, she didn't have any fresh clothes to change into, so her choice was to either look like a slob in James's pajamas or smell like a gym locker in her sweaty running clothes. This was typical of James—sweet to want her to stay but blind to the reality that his parents were going to judge her. And even though his bathroom was irritatingly neat, his shampoo situation was pathetic.

They could tell the news wasn't good when they came back from their run and James's family just stared at them in silence. Cody quickly excused herself to shower and hid behind the rush of hot water for at least twenty minutes. When Cody felt like she was starting to be rude, she finally got out of the shower and caught her reflection in the mirror. *Fine*, she conceded with a bit of pride. She could understand why some people were jealous. The high cheekbones, the perfect symmetry, the tasteful constellation of freckles—she knew she was truly beautiful. But Cody reminded herself that it was not as if she or anyone else had asked for this. It was just how they were born. It was who they were.

Cody, James, and hundreds of thousands of other kids across the country were pioneers, the first babies born with the benefits of advanced genetic engineering. All of them were sanctioned by a pilot program run by the National Institutes of Health, which agreed to study this new technology by granting permission to a small segment of the population. One percent, to be exact.

For the past twenty years, one out of every hundred newborn babies had been genetically engineered. A scientist had manipulated their genomes, selecting certain traits from their parents and eliminating others. *Grocery shopping*, it was called. It was no surprise, then, that Cody, James, and their fellow participants were tall, sturdy athletes with perfect facial features.

Actually, it was still a surprise to Cody: She couldn't believe that her meager gene pool had offered any positive traits to choose from. Between her wonderful but entirely average mother and what little she knew about her father, the scientists didn't have a lot to work with. But clearly they'd found something, because here she was, just as perfectly assembled as all the other Ones, as they had come to be known. Sometimes the magnitude of her good fortune took her breath away—literally had her gasping for air. Who was she to deserve such a fate? No one, really, just one baby out of a hundred, chosen by a random government lottery. How would she be able to pay this gift back? And to whom and when and where? Cody thought about this constantly, but she still didn't have an answer.

Being a One was obviously a gift, she knew that much. The benefits bestowed by this new technology were easy to see, and besides the good looks and physical advantages, it could eradicate any negative trait, from asthma to acne. The unforeseen drawbacks, however, were still being understood. Sure, the children in the study were perfectly healthy and wholly human. But as this first generation reached adulthood, the rest of the world was starting to take notice.

The Ones were excelling. Even in preschool, it was easy to guess which toddlers were part of the trial. As Cody toweled off her hair one more time and continued to stall, she thought back fondly to those early days of playing tag, when no one could catch her, and some of the other kids couldn't even run without toppling over. Now the oldest Ones were having an impact on the world. Several of James and Cody's peers had gone on to remarkable accomplishments for people so young: graduating from college early; winning Olympic medals; starting successful businesses; making an impact in the arts, music, and science. It was clear that they had been born with a tremendous advantage.

As Cody stepped into the carpeted hallway, she heard the TV droning from the living room downstairs. She shivered, knowing all too well what the yelling was about.

A grassroots organization called the Equality Movement had taken hold of the country with the stated goal of ensuring fair and equal rights for every citizen. But what they really wanted, Cody knew, was to persecute the Ones. And it seemed that with Amber Reed, a sweet little cheerleader from South Carolina, they had found an ingenious way to do it.

The snowball that turned into an avalanche started with poor Amber getting cut from her freshman cheerleading team. Amber's parents sued the school, alleging that the Ones who were selected to the team had an illegal advantage. Leaders from the Equality Movement seized on this lawsuit, identifying it as a perfect vessel to challenge the very existence of the Ones. The Cheerleader Case eventually turned into *Reed v. The National Institutes of Health*, and Amber's spot on the team was no longer the central issue—instead, the Supreme Court was about to decide if genetic engineering was actually legal. The Equality Movement had played its hand perfectly. And while Cody and James were out running, the decision had come down.

Genetic engineering had been declared illegal.

Cody, James, and all the others now lived on an island in history, with no one like them having come before and none allowed to come after—an orphaned generation. It was a lonely feeling, and it prompted Cody to finally get dressed and go downstairs.

═

Dinner was exactly what Cody had expected. James's mom, Helen, was layered as usual in three different sweaters and a stack of bangle bracelets. She refused to sit for more than two seconds, constantly popping up to bring in food or to clear away plates. And God forbid if a crumb hit the floor. James's father perched at the head of the table and directed the conversation by peering over his narrow spectacles. Arthur was a professor at the state university nearby, and he asked Cody for the tenth time what she planned to study in college.

"Costume design," she answered, running out of random professions that she knew would drive Arthur crazy.

"Interesting," he said, trying not to choke on his food. "Sounds colorful."

"Totally," Cody replied, glancing at James and suppressing a smile. She felt him flick her knee under the table.

And then there was Michael, James's brother. He was six years older, tall, handsome, and dark-haired like James and wearing a similarly boring button-down shirt. He had graduated from college and worked as an engineer for a while but recently had to move back home. Michael had been quiet for most of the meal, but Cody saw him put his fork down deliberately and turn to her and James.

"What did you think of the court's decision today?" he asked.

"Michael, come on—" James started to say.

"Do you agree with it or not?"

Cody saw James look to his father, but Arthur also seemed curious to hear an answer.

"I get that people are nervous about what will happen eventually," James said, "but that's the case with all new technology. It doesn't mean you should ban it."

"Easy for you to say," Michael said. He turned to Cody. "What about you?"

"It's total bullshit," she said, then looked over at James's mom, feeling bad about the cursing. Helen wiped her mouth with a napkin, as if she were the one who had said it. Meanwhile, Michael was smiling, clearly pleased that he'd provoked such a response. Cody felt James touch her leg again, but she knocked his hand away.

"I know you agree with me," Cody said to Michael. "You're just too scared to admit it. Stopping scientific progress just because a bunch of old people are afraid of losing their jobs is ridiculous."

The whole family jerked their eyes toward her, and Cody knew right away that she had put her foot in her mouth. She had forgotten for a second that Michael had just lost his job to a younger, more talented engineer. He suspected that his replacement was a One.

"I'm sorry," Cody said sincerely. "I just don't think banning the science helps anyone. There are always going to be younger people moving into professions, whether they are Ones or not."

"The court disagrees—they ruled nine to zero. And Congress is about to pass more laws that address the Ones' unfair advantages," Michael said.

"Unfair advantages?" Cody repeated. "That's nothing new. What about being born into a rich family? Being delivered by good doctors in a fancy hospital? Having a parent at home who has time to read to you? Pretty nice, I bet. Should the court make laws so that none of that is unfair?"

"There's obviously a line somewhere. The vast majority of the country knows that we've gone too far," Michael said.

"I wonder why," James chimed in, trying to deflect some attention away from Cody.

"Don't give me that crap about you guys being a poor little minority group," his brother replied.

"What are we, then?" Cody said, jumping back in. "We have no political power, no leadership, no money, no way to defend our rights, and we are outnumbered ninety-nine to one."

"That's exactly what the Equality Movement is all about—making sure everyone has the *same* rights," Michael said.

"The Equality Movement wants to take away our rights," Cody shot back. "They want to get rid of us."

"No, we don't," Michael responded. "We just want—"

"*We?*" Helen said quickly, surprising everyone at the table. She was normally so quiet it was easy to forget that she was there. "Since when are you part of the Equality Movement?"

Michael sat silently for a moment, startled by his mother's intensity. Helen reached out and grabbed each of her sons by the shoulder.

"This is your brother! You don't ever do anything to harm him. Neither of you. Ever!"

Immediately, Cody realized what was behind Helen's uncharacteristic outburst. This wasn't about Michael or James; this was about Helen's other son, the one who had passed away. Cody didn't know much about him, only that he had died before James was born. Maybe that version of the family had been different, perhaps better, in a way. It was still two parents and two sons, but at least in the original version, the brothers were on equal footing. This current dynamic wasn't James's fault, Cody knew. But maybe the rest of his family didn't.

Back at the table, Michael mumbled an apology. Helen let go of her boys, collected herself, and went into the kitchen. Then Cody watched as James and Michael looked at each other across the table, and the moment almost shattered her. She saw the truth in their eyes—ceaseless adoration on one side, implacable jealousy on the other—and she knew they would never really be brothers. Not while Michael saw James only as a One. Not while he saw him as a replacement.

=

Even though Cody wanted to walk by herself, James insisted on driving her home, so they climbed into the beat-up red Jeep that James refused to let die. To his credit, he could work wonders on an engine. Did he just learn that one day? Or was he programmed from birth to fix a leaky carburetor? These were the types of questions that Cody had to ask herself whenever she was good at something. Was she *born* this way, or was she *made* this way? Should the difference even matter?

"I'm sorry," James said as they pulled out of the driveway. "I know that was awkward."

"It's fine," Cody said. "*You* didn't do anything wrong."

"Michael doesn't really mean that stuff. He's just dealing with a tough break right now."

"He has a One in his own family, and he still can't stand us. Can you imagine what everyone else is thinking right now?"

"No one is thinking anything. Everything is fine."

"When are you going to wake up?" Cody snapped, louder than she'd meant to. James shrank back in his seat, surprised at her eruption. "This court decision is just the beginning. Who knows what law will pass next week, or a month from now? Someone spat on the ground when I walked past the other day. Why would a person do that?" she asked, and then answered, "Because they're making it legal to hate us."

"Calm down. This was the law that the Equality Movement wanted. They're getting it. Now it's over."

Cody shook her head, frustrated by how naive James was being. "Maybe if I put this in terms you can actually understand . . ."

"Go right ahead."

"Remember when we started dating, and I wouldn't let you kiss me?"

"Of course," James said. "It was diabolical." He couldn't help a cute half smile at the thought, but Cody wasn't going to be distracted.

"And then after we kissed, what happened?"

20

"You saw stars and realized you could never live without me?" He beamed a full smile at her.

"You wish. I mean the next time we hooked up, what happened?" Cody pulled one of his arms from the steering wheel and waved it in front of his face. "With these things."

"My hands? Oh. They, uh, wanted to move around."

"Exactly. And then what? After they had 'moved around' a few times?"

"They wanted to do other things." He said with the beginning of a blush creeping onto his cheeks.

"And so on and so forth, each step meeting less resistance than the one before it," Cody said.

James was finally grasping her point. "Wow. So all the Ones are going to be marched off to their deaths?"

"Pretty much," Cody responded, pleased with her lesson.

"Because you let me kiss you in the stacks of the library that day?"

Cody smacked him hard in the chest, and James laughed, trying to block it. "I am being serious here!" she yelled.

"I know, I know, I'm sorry," he said as he slowed the car down in front of Cody's house. "But honestly, I swear, I don't think we have anything to worry about." He put the car into park and turned it off.

Cody gave him a weird look. "What are you doing?"

"I'm coming in. You can't possibly go through that

whole analogy and expect me not to hang out for a few minutes."

"That wasn't my point."

James took his hands off the steering wheel and held them harmlessly up in the air. "Hands at ten and two, I promise," he said, smiling.

Cody tried to stay angry with him, but it was impossible with his hands raised in mock innocence, his dimples deep enough to have dimples of their own. And then there was the dark hair that tumbled over his forehead, the curls thick enough to have curls of their own. James had a way of looking at her that made the hair on the back of her neck stand up and dance.

"Fine," she finally said, knowing she didn't have the willpower to resist. "My mom's already asleep anyway."

They got out of the Jeep and walked quietly up to the small clapboard house. Cody silently unlocked the door, and they tiptoed through the dark, cramped living room and into Cody's bedroom. James banged into a chair in her room and had to stifle a groan. They tried not to step on the broken microscopes and old doctor bags that littered the floor. Cody turned on a globe that threw stars across the wall, making it a little easier to see.

"You okay?" she asked.

James sat down on the bed and pulled her down next to him. "Couldn't be better," he said.

Cody turned to face him and hovered there for a

moment, savoring that sensation of being close enough to feel someone without actually touching. And then, finally, barely having to move, they pressed their lips together.

After a second or two, James pulled back a few inches. "PQ3318," he said.

Cody smiled. "PQ3318," she answered back.

That was the library catalog code that James had written on a scrap of paper and handed to her before disappearing into the stacks. When she got up the courage to actually go look for him, it had taken forever to find him, the butterflies inside her getting crazier with each step. The random book he had picked was deep in their cavernous library, and when she finally walked down the right aisle, they were totally alone. "I almost gave up on—" he had started to say, but Cody didn't let him finish. PQ3318 was their secret.

It was a wonderful memory, and Cody relished it as she reached up to touch James's face and kissed him again. Their bodies pushed into each other, heating up as articles of clothing began to come off.

And that was when the brick crashed through her window.

Cody gasped as hundreds of glass shards exploded over their heads. Her bed was directly below the window that now had a gaping hole in it.

"Stay down," James yelled, but Cody crawled to the window and shoved her face out between the jagged edges.

She caught a glimpse of a car, which shot off into the night, tires squealing, lights off, a faint shout of triumph drifting back down the empty street.

She turned to James, who was standing in shock. "Are you all right?" he asked.

Cody didn't answer. She looked down at the glass-strewn comforter and went to pick up the brick off the floor. It was solid, heavy, cold. Then she turned it over in her hands and saw it.

Two parallel lines, painted in white to stand out against the red brick—a perfectly drawn equal sign. As Cody looked at it, she wasn't fearful or angry or nervous. To her surprise, she felt something entirely different. She felt . . . ready.

Cody held up the brick to show James, her arms steady, eyes clear. "I told you this was just the beginning."

CHAPTER 2

JAMES STOOD DUMBSTRUCK as Cody showed him the brick. He saw the equal sign and knew what it meant. Yet all he could think to say was, "Watch out for the broken glass."

Broken glass was easy enough to deal with; you watched where you stepped and then swept it up. James was always finding the most efficient way to proceed, and there was a beautiful logic to this problem: Broken glass was dangerous, so you cleaned it up carefully. A brick flying at their heads was another matter. James didn't have a solution for that. Cody did, though. *Of course she does*, James thought, and from the look on her face, it didn't involve a broom.

"Let's go," she said, eyes aflame. "I saw their car."

Cody grabbed a sweatshirt and bounded out of her room. James felt his adrenaline pumping, too. He knew it was a natural biological reaction, a step in the fight-or-flight proccss. And he knew just as well that he landed squarely on the *flight* side. But to where? The whole country had heard the Supreme Court ruling by now, and they were all wearing the requisite LET AMBER CHEER! bracelets. If people were blowing off steam by throwing bricks at Ones, then chasing after this car didn't seem like the best idea.

"Come on!" Cody loudly whispered from the hallway, and James knew there was no use in arguing with her. Quite literally, she wasn't even there to argue with, so he had no choice but to follow her outside, moving carefully back through the dark living room and easing the front door shut behind him. Cody was waiting for him next to his Jeep.

"How did your mom not hear that?" he asked.

"Sound machine, sleeping mask, earplugs—that woman would sleep through the apocalypse."

James got in the car and unlocked the doors so Cody could hop into the passenger's seat. She was still holding the brick. "What are you going to do with that?"

"I'm not sure yet," she said, setting it on her lap. "Drive to the quarry, and we'll figure it out."

James had the key in the ignition, ready to start the car, but he paused and gave her a questioning look. *The quarry? How did she know where to go?*

Cody reached over and grabbed his hand. James took

solace in it for a moment . . . until Cody twisted the key and brought the engine to life.

$$=$$

If there was anything good about being raised in the town of Shasta, the quarry in the abandoned mine—long since filled with water—was at the top, middle, and end of the list. It was a gigantic playground where the local kids grew up swimming in the deep reservoir, climbing the smooth sandstone walls, and daring each other to jump off the cliffs. It made for a glorious way to spend a summer day, and the fact that it was sealed off and you needed to sneak in gave it just the right feeling of danger. More than 150 years had passed since the last gold miners had stripped the mountain bare, but the various tunnels, chutes, and pathways they had carved were still present. Of course, they were hard to see now, and every local campfire legend involved some poor kid falling down an unexpected hole and slowly transforming into a grizzled maniac who terrorized the town. This never really scared James; even as a little kid, he knew that gold mines were not dug down in straight vertical shafts and that you couldn't just fall into one.

But the real reason James had never worried about falling into a tunnel was that he had been to the quarry only once in his life.

That wasn't normal for a Shasta kid, but James's parents made it clear that this was their firmest rule. He had defied them once, hiked up with his friends when he was ten or eleven and had the time of his life making perfect dives from the highest perches. When his mother found out, she slapped him across the face. Hard, angrily, violently. It was the only time his parents had ever touched him, and the sheer surprise of it made him sob instantly. He could always recall the exact details of that moment, the warm sensation of blood surging to his temple, the sting on his cheek, the look in his mom's eyes that somehow made him feel like he deserved it.

And maybe he did deserve it, he figured out a few years later. When he was old enough to finally put the full picture together, he realized that his brother had drowned at the quarry. Thomas, the sibling he had never met. The child that James was meant to replace. So he came to understand how it must have been great news to his parents when they were selected for the NIH pilot program and told that their newly conceived embryo was eligible to be genetically engineered. It was a miracle—not only could they replace Thomas, but they could also guarantee that their new child would be just as perfect.

James felt that pressure every day of his life. Long ago, he realized that he could never screw up. Never get in trouble, never disappoint, never drown in some senseless accident. James had internalized these expectations and worked his ass off to meet them every day. It had made him cautious, thoughtful, and reserved. He was the president of his class at school, the captain of the debate team, a tireless dishwasher at home—doing a damn good job of being perfect, he thought. But for some people, he was starting to realize, it would never be enough.

So maybe it was good that he was here right now, driving through the dark on this winding road to the place where he was never supposed to go. He wasn't scared; he was excited. Curious, too. He loved being in the wilderness, and if he weren't so overwhelmed with chores and activities, he'd happily hike around the woods all day long. But James could barely remember what the quarry was like from that one visit, and he knew it would be different at night. He also knew that people went there to party sometimes, but he had never been. He looked over at Cody.

"Have you been up here at night before?" he asked.

She hesitated for a moment. "Once or twice maybe."

"Like for a party?"

Cody squinted as she saw something ahead of them and then gestured to a spot in the woods. "Over there," she said. "There's an old dirt road behind those bushes."

James slowed down and pulled to the side. He slid through some undergrowth and then started down a bumpy road with branches clawing at their windows. At the end of it, he could make out the faint glow of a bonfire. Cody pointed to a little clearing off the path, and James steered the Jeep into the small area that was hidden from the road.

He shut the car off and turned to Cody. "What now?" he asked.

"Someone owes us an apology."

Cody hopped out of the car, brick still in hand, and started toward the bonfire. James walked next to her, taking in the heavy darkness and trying to force his eyes to adjust. Sure, he had perfect vision, but he still couldn't see in the dark. There was music playing ahead of them, kids shouting, shadows dancing through the bright orange flames. Looking on from a distance, James immediately felt inclined to give everyone a lecture on fire safety. He had been an ace fire starter in his Boy Scout troop, and that included learning all the dangers that came with camping in a prehistoric, dry pine forest. The sparks rising from the bonfire ahead practically gave him a heart attack. One unlucky change in the wind could burn down half the state.

Cody and James pressed forward, and when they reached the end of the path, James finally got his bearings. Ahead of them—or really below them—was the expansive reservoir, black, shiny, and still in the calm night. They had emerged to stand on top of a giant cliff, carved smooth and flat up to its edge, sixty feet over the water. And they had stepped right into a scene that even James had to admit seemed like an awesome party.

"Yooooooo!" someone shouted, finally noticing them. "You're hella late!"

James and Cody stepped into the light, closer to the oil-barrel trash can containing the flames. About thirty people from their school were milling around. James recognized most of them but didn't exactly see any friends. And whoever had shouted at them changed his tone when he saw Cody and James.

"Oh," he said. "You guys lost or something?"

James saw who was talking to them: a kid named Marco Spiller, the de facto leader of the Bench Mob. The Bench was a noted landmark at their school, an otherwise boring piece of public infrastructure that happened to be set in concrete just on the other side of the school's property line. It was technically off-campus, and thus a convenient meeting spot for any activity that wasn't allowed on school grounds. There were always kids gathered around the Bench, but only a few actually sat down on it. Marco Spiller perched on it like it was a throne.

He continued eyeing James and Cody and then began to smile. "Or did you guys come to party?"

All of a sudden, from the corner of his eye, James saw a burst of sparks. He turned just in time to see a kid vault over the garbage can, jumping straight through the fire and landing right in front of them.

"Ain't no party like a quarry party, 'cause a quarry party got *rocks*!" the kid shouted, and then fell over laughing as everyone else whooped and hollered. This was Fitz. If Marco was the king of the Bench Mob, Fitz was the

jester. The rest of their crew was there, too, all in varia-
tions of their uniform—thick jeans, flannel shirts, base-
ball hats with flat brims tilted at odd angles.

James instinctively took a step closer to Cody, but she
wasn't there anymore. She had walked right up to Marco.

"Is that your car?" she asked, pointing at the beat-up
Mazda coupe that had been pulled up to the edge of the
cliff and was blasting music for the party.

"We found that here," Marco said. "Lucky, huh?"

"That car drove past my house tonight."

"Impossible. We've been up here all night. It hasn't
moved an inch."

"Truth," Fitz chimed in. "Although I went to piss a few
times, so maybe it moved then."

"What's that?" Marco said, reaching and taking the
brick from Cody's hands.

"You tell me," she said.

Marco turned the brick over in his hands, tracing his
fingers over the equal sign. "Looks like some kind of message. Like a warning to gennies or something." He paused.
"You are a genny, right?"

James bristled at Marco's word choice. For some people,
genny was the preferred slur to refer to kids who had been
genetically engineered. James felt the urge to sucker-punch
Marco right there, but he knew the fallout from that
momentary satisfaction wouldn't be worth it.

"A One? Yeah, I am," Cody said proudly.

"I thought so," Marco said. "Bad day to be a One, huh?"

"Real bad," Fitz said. "I heard they're gonna stuff all of them in the Grand Canyon and throw away the key." Fitz cackled, and James just felt bad for him. If anyone could have used a genetic boost, it was this degenerate.

Then Fitz stepped closer to Cody, looked her over, and turned to Marco. "But I didn't know they let poor people be Ones."

"It was decided by random lottery, you idiot," Cody said.

"I guess rich people are just better at lotteries, then," Marco replied, and turned to look at James for the first time. Well, for the first time that night. James and Marco had looked each other square in the eye many times before. That's what happened when you were the two best athletes growing up together in a small town. They had always been matched up against each other, both of them so skilled at every sport that the only way to make fair teams was to have them cancel each other out. That's how every school yard football game and driveway basketball game had played out for years, James and Marco going at each other tooth and nail and playing to a standstill. James had actually started to enjoy their battles and relished the rare opportunity to compete against an equal. But then Marco quit playing sports. They hadn't faced off for years now.

As Marco stared at James, Cody snatched the brick

back from him. "If you've got a message for me, you can say it to my face," she said.

Marco's slick smile returned. "Take it easy—this wasn't from me. I'm down with you gennies. I mean, you people. In fact, you should stay and hang out, have some fun."

James caught Cody's eye and saw her confusion. Neither of them believed Marco, but what could they say?

Marco continued talking to Cody. "Now you, I know I've seen you up here before," he said with a knowing smirk. Then he turned to James. "But you . . . this is your first time, right?"

"Yeah," James replied. "So what?"

"Well, if you want to stay at a quarry party, you've got to initiate."

"Initiate?"

Marco gestured to the edge of the cliff. "Leap of faith, bro, and then you're cool to stay. We all did it."

James heard several people in the crowd give their assent. He looked over to the darkness beyond the cliff. He knew it was just water below—deep, calm, clear water—but he had no interest in confirming that. And even if the water seemed tranquil, he knew it wasn't. That water had the power to kill, to hurt not just the people who went in it but also people miles away and years removed. Maybe there was a grain of truth in the campfire legends: A boy could disappear into this quarry and end up tormenting the people he left behind.

James stopped looking at the reservoir and turned to Cody. "Come on, let's go." He started walking toward her, but Marco stepped in his way.

"I'm not jumping. We don't even want to stay," he said to Marco.

James tried to walk around him, but Marco cut him off again. He was blocking James from getting to Cody. Then Fitz and a couple of other guys stepped over. They formed a semicircle around James, with his back to the edge of the cliff now. Slowly, they pressed forward.

"What's wrong, James? Aren't you a One?" Marco asked pointedly. "Ones can do all kinds of cool stuff, right? You guys can probably even fly."

Marco and his buddies tightened into a circle. James had no choice but to take a step back. He wasn't on the edge yet, but there wasn't much room left. He considered his options: jump on his own, which didn't sound very appealing, or rush these guys, try to fight them off, and maybe end up falling over regardless. At least he'd bring a few down with him, he thought, grasping for a silver lining. It was hard to think. The music was loud, people around the fire were shouting, and Marco was inching closer. James steadied himself, ready to charge.

And then, out of nowhere, there was the tremendous sound of glass shattering. It was followed by dead silence. The music had stopped abruptly, and no one spoke.

Everyone on the cliff looked over to where Marco's car

was parked. Cody stood in front of the hood, having quite obviously just thrown the brick through the car's windshield. She stared defiantly at Marco.

"Now we're even."

The mayhem that followed lasted only a few seconds, but James felt as if he watched every event unfold in slow motion. First, the pure anger that came across Marco's face, then the speed at which he charged Cody. Marco yelled something at her, something horrible, then grabbed the burning trash can. James saw that Cody was trying to join him on the edge of the cliff, and if she could make it, he knew that they could get out of there, that the crowd of people penning him in had dispersed enough to let them squeeze through. And finally, as she ran toward him, James saw Marco lift the trash can over his shoulder and hurl it at Cody.

The burning missile landed directly in front of her, the metal screeching on the rock, sparks and half-burned logs bouncing off the ground. James watched the embers shoot up into Cody's face, saw the look of panic and searing pain, and saw her balance start to shift. With two more strides, she would have been next to him, and he could have caught her, but she never made it. The fiery trash can bounced right in her path and sent her tumbling off the cliff.

James watched her fall, watched as Cody disappeared into total darkness. He stood on the edge, trying to see, straining to hear. There was a splash and then nothing but silence. Silence in the quarry, and silence from everyone behind him. And somehow the silence helped James focus, helped him translate the moment into a straight-forward problem-and-solution format with an answer that was obvious, even if it contradicted every physical instinct in his body. The equation was simple: Cody had fallen into the darkness, and he had to help her.

So he jumped.

CHAPTER 3

AS CODY TWISTED through the air high over the reservoir, she waited desperately to hit the water. She didn't care if the impact would hurt, if she would drown or freeze to death or get devoured by a giant squid. All she cared about was getting the fire out of her eyes, the burning embers that had bounced up into her face and left her with a searing blindness. The sixty-foot free fall into the water couldn't end soon enough.

Of course, falling in total darkness while completely blind made for a brutal landing. Cody hit the water with a violent thud that immediately knocked the wind out of her. Instead of calmly holding her breath like every other time she'd dived into the quarry, Cody felt the need to breathe right away. But she was sinking, and her baggy sweatshirt was riding up over her shoulders and tangling her arms. She tried to swim upward, but it was no use; every attempted motion just made the straitjacket even tighter. She had to take a breath—her brain demanded it—so she opened her mouth and gasped for air, but got only water. This made her panic even more, and she continued flailing helplessly in her heavy, twisted clothing, sinking deeper and deeper. At least her eyes had stopped burning.

Then a hand touched her, clawed at her face, and started to pull her—first painfully by the hair, then from under her shoulder—and with great force she was dragged to the surface, and she knew that James had found her.

When they finally exploded out of the water, Cody gasped and coughed and inhaled all at once, which actually served no purpose at all. But her second inhale worked a little better, and she devoured the cold, clear air, drawing huge breaths and finally freeing herself from her anchor of a sweatshirt. She sensed James floating beside her—couldn't see him in the moonless night, but heard him taking the same gigantic breaths. As Cody strained to locate him, she realized why this moment felt so incredibly surreal.

She had never seen James swim before.

"Can you make it to the rocks?" he said, his voice cutting through the darkness.

"Yes," she replied, and they started paddling slowly to the edge of the water. When they reached a low rock shelf, they pulled themselves up and lay still for a moment. Unable to talk, Cody took James's hand and held it against her pounding heart. From there they would have to find one of the rocky staircases that led back to the top of the quarry. Traipse through the woods and locate their car. Avoid Marco and the other idiots if possible. And drive back down the mountain, back to where this whole night had started. But for now they lay motionless, staring out over the black water as it rippled almost imperceptibly.

Cody turned toward James, not knowing where to begin.

"Did they push you off, too?" she asked.

James hesitated for a moment, then answered softly. "No. I jumped."

And with that the tears came at once, in an overwhelming rush, and Cody pulled James closer and held on as tight as she could.

=

Cody was dragging the next morning as she waited to board the bus to school. She usually sat with her friend Erica, a human jolt of caffeine who lived down the street from her. Of course, Erica had already pounced as they waited on the sidewalk.

"I heard what happened at the quarry last night. Now tell me *everything*," she said.

Cody didn't have the energy for this. "You just said you heard already."

"Not from you! Now, spill it."

They got on the bus, and Cody slid into a seat alone. She looked up at Erica. "Sorry, E, I think I just need to sleep this morning." She pulled her hood over her head and tried to get comfortable.

But as the bus rumbled along the pockmarked street, Cody couldn't help staring out the window at all the new flags that had cropped up, the crisp equal signs flapping proudly in the breeze. And then there was the traffic jam in the center of town, as everyone rubbernecked past the flower shop, with its shattered windows and walls charred with smoke from a fire the week before. An accident, perhaps. Maybe it had nothing to do with the fact that the florist's son was a One, a quiet, friendly boy named Victor in the grade below her.

So Cody was already on edge in her first-period English class when the announcement came over the PA system. It was odd for a class to be interrupted like this, and as Margie, the ancient school secretary, started talking, Cody noticed her voice wasn't as sunny as usual.

"Will the following students please report to the office immediately . . ."

Everyone looked up at the speakers expectantly as the names were rattled off slowly and formally. Cody Bell. James Livingston. Then all the rest of the Ones in school, around ten in total. When Margie was done, Cody felt her classmates turn their attention from the speakers to her. As she moved toward the door, she desperately wanted someone to lighten the moment, to make a joke about getting to miss class or to ask her to bring back some candy from the giant bowl on Margie's desk. But instead they all silently watched her, and each gaze seemed to say the same thing: *I'm glad I'm not her.*

Cody joined the rest of the Ones in the office and immediately felt weird seeing all of them in one place. It's not like the Ones socialized only with each other; that would hardly be feasible, considering there were just a few of them in each grade. Plus, there was never any official moment when a kid was publicly declared a One. In fact, there was nothing that even required parents to tell their child that he or she had been genetically engineered. And it wasn't like you could simply tell from looking. There were plenty of people at school who were healthy and good-looking and athletic, but that didn't mean they were Ones. Inevitably, though, word got around, and it became common knowledge in their town and school and clearly with the principal about who was a One. Cody and the others had always shared an extra look or smile in the hallways. They were a tiny slice of the population, so of course a bond existed between them. And now that shared bond had landed them all in the school office.

"What do you think this is about?" a hulking senior

named Gregory asked. He was a gentle giant, the star of the football team, and not used to being in trouble.

Cody shrugged, not knowing for sure and not too excited to find out.

They took seats and leaned against walls in the waiting area, staring at the closed office door of Principal Bixley. Ms. Bixley kept them waiting, the school day passing by around them, other students walking by and staring at them like animals in a zoo. Cody grew frustrated, knowing she was missing her chemistry lab now, where she had been looking forward to messing around with some liquid nitrogen. At least sweet old Margie shuffled around with her candy bowl at one point and whispered an apology. Cody smiled at her, trying not to make her feel bad. Other than that, they waited silently.

When Ms. Bixley finally emerged, she had the usual fake smile plastered on her face. Cody had always felt that Ms. Bixley was petty and calculating, but apparently her trick worked on other people. She was young for a principal and carried herself with an eager but serious manner, like the daughter of a president, a perfect angel who had never made a mistake.

"I hope you weren't waiting long," she said.

"Why are we here?" Cody asked, not able to take it any longer.

"I'd love to explain, Cody, if you'll let me," Ms. Bixley said cheerfully. "I'm sure some of you are a little anxious about the Supreme Court decision yesterday. It seems to have triggered some unintended and ugly consequences across the country, and I'd be nervous, too, if I were in your shoes. I understand, sadly, that even Shasta is feeling the effects of this new atmosphere, and I'm sorry to hear that many of your homes were vandalized last night."

Cody jolted up, surprised. Apparently, she wasn't the only One who'd had a brick shatter her window. It made her feel better and worse at the same time. She turned to James, who was leaning against the wall next to her. They hadn't talked since he'd taken her home after the quarry. She mouthed a question to him, and he shook his head—his house hadn't been hit.

"In light of these events," Ms. Bixley continued, "we want you to know that we will do everything in our power here at school to preserve a safe, welcoming environment. To ensure that, we have decided to give all of you special school ID cards. Margie?"

Ms. Bixley reached out to Margie, who scurried around her desk with several lanyard necklaces attached to plastic ID tags. Ms. Bixley took them and started to walk around the room, holding each necklace open and placing it over the head of every student as if they were part of some sad Olympic-medal ceremony.

"We've put sensors on the school doors, and these cards will let us know when you enter and exit all the buildings. That way, if there's any trouble, or if your parents are looking for you or something else comes up, we'll always know exactly where you are. Just make sure to wear them at all times!" she explained.

When Ms. Bixley got to her, Cody didn't bow her head. "I'm not wearing a tracking collar."

"It's for your own protection, Cody, and it's not a choice. You won't be allowed in school without one." She reached up again to fit the lanyard over Cody's head, but Cody grabbed it from her quickly and stuffed it into her fraying jeans.

"Then I'll keep it in my pocket." Cody glared at Ms. Bixley but just got that same wide smile in return.

"All right, then, back to class, everyone." She held her gaze on Cody. "And stay safe."

—

Cody sat through her next class in a fog of anger, the ID card burning a hole in her pocket. Sure, every student had a school ID that they used to check out library books and register for classes and things like that. And if the Ones and their families and their property were in danger, Cody understood the need for precautions. But Ms. Bixley's insistence that they wear the IDs around their necks drove her crazy. That wasn't a safety measure; it was a scarlet letter, a piece of plastic that practically screamed out the word *genny*.

When her history class ended, Cody started to file out with everyone else, but her teacher waved her over.

Mr. Oberlee rarely got up from his desk, which was understandable considering that he was shaped like a penguin and equally unsuited for walking on land. Yet somehow Mr. Oberlee also coached the cross-country team, an irony that had always delighted Cody. She thought he was the best teacher in the school and even enjoyed his passionate reenactments of Winston Churchill speeches, so she let him slide on being clueless about the bio-mechanics of long-distance running.

"Hi, Cody, I wanted to catch you before practice. I imagine you're pretty excited for the meet on Friday?" Mr. Oberlee said.

"Of course," she said. Even more than running on her own, Cody loved the chess match of the actual competition. Her main tactic was to bolt hard right from the start, making the rest of the pack nervous and forcing them to exert themselves too early. But the smarter girls stalked her, assuming that Cody would eventually fade. Cody's secret was that she always saved a hidden gear for the final stretch and would open her stride when the other runners made their move. She loved seeing the surprise on their faces when she let loose—loved imagining it, rather, because she never actually saw their faces.

"As you know, we can only enter five runners in the race," Mr. Oberlee continued. "And I thought that this week might be a good chance to give some of the other girls a shot."

"I don't understand," Cody said, genuinely not following him.

"You're not going to run this week."

"But I'm our fastest runner."

"I know that. And I get that this might seem unfair. To be honest, I don't like it, either," he said, looking down and then out the window, and Cody could tell that this ridiculous idea hadn't originated with Mr. Oberlee.

"Then why can't I run?" she asked.

"Because, well, that's just how it has to be this week," he said, and started fiddling with some papers. "I'm sorry, Cody."

Cody stumbled out of the classroom, crushed about not being able to run, but even angrier about the new reality that she had to acknowledge: *Reed v. NIH* had changed things. Technically speaking, it applied only to banning the technology for future generations, but practically speaking, the whole world was against her now. Maybe they always had been, but now they had permission from the government. And as she walked into the cafeteria for lunch, Cody discovered that she wasn't the only One suffering for it.

A group of Ones was gathered around a single table. *Weird*, Cody thought, to see the Ones from different grades all together like that again—and to her irritation, all of them had their ID draped around their neck. The group huddled around Laura, who was sobbing. Cody had never liked Laura and thought she was an entitled brat who worried too much about matching her nail polish to her scarf. But Laura did seem genuinely distraught, so Cody sat down and tried to catch up.

"*Understudy?* He actually said I could still be the *understudy*!" Laura squealed, with tears and saliva falling onto her magenta silk blouse and skinny jeans. *So much for that outfit*, Cody thought. She made eye contact with James, and he walked around the table and knelt down next to her.

"She lost the lead in the musical. The drama teacher gave the part to somebody else," James said, filling in the blanks. "And the same thing happened to me. I was supposed to deliver the final rebuttal for our debate team tomorrow. But our faculty adviser just told me I'm out. No explanation at all."

The rest of the Ones each had a similar story, but Cody barely needed to hear them. She saw all too clearly that a systematic policy had been implemented to take away everything the Ones had earned. Cody stood up and bolted into the hall, heading for Ms. Bixley's office.

She barged straight through the waiting area, past Margie, and through the principal's door. "I know this is all your idea," Cody accused her.

Ms. Bixley smiled, as if she was pleased at Cody's agitation. "Is something wrong?"

Cody could have flipped over her desk right then, but

she had already used up the benefit of the doubt when it came to suspicious acts of violence against Ms. Bixley. During last year's homecoming weekend, Cody and her teammates had been warming up for their soccer game. Behind the field, Ms. Bixley was at the bake sale, and with a ball at her feet, Cody couldn't resist ripping a shot in Ms. Bixley's direction with the vague intention of startling her or knocking some cookies off the table. To Cody's surprise and secret satisfaction, the soccer ball bounced squarely off Ms. Bixley's face, and the blood that gushed out of her nose ruined every last baked good. Cody had apologized, of course, and the whole thing was written off as an accident, but any reasonable person who saw the location of the soccer goal might have drawn a different conclusion. Regardless, Cody knew she probably couldn't get away with injuring Ms. Bixley a second time. So she tried her best to be civil.

"You are kicking the Ones out of the positions they earned," Cody said. She assumed Ms. Bixley would deny it or play dumb, but her answer made Cody even angrier.

"Of course we are. It's a new day, Cody, and everyone is focused on equality right now. The Supreme Court, Congress, the Board of Education—they all think it best if we are a little more vigilant about giving everyone equal opportunities. I'm just following their new guidelines. Don't you think it's fair for those other students to get a chance?"

"Not if they don't deserve it. And not if they're worse."

"*Deserve?* Did the first group of students *deserve* it? Or were they just more fortunate?"

Cody saw where Ms. Bixley was going: She was implying that the Ones hadn't earned their accomplishments. Cody understood the logic, but in her case it just wasn't true. Yeah, she was born with long legs and a strong heart, but those abilities were still totally organic to her. In fact, they might have existed no matter how she was born. There was no way to know, and Cody couldn't stand being punished for that.

"What if you got fired because the school hired someone less qualified?" Cody asked. "Would that seem fair to you?"

"I earned this job. Through hard work and my God-given abilities," Ms. Bixley said. "It wasn't bestowed upon me in a petri dish."

Cody stared back at her, wishing she had a soccer ball. Then Ms. Bixley walked over to stand right in front of her. There was a different look on her face; she had dropped the perfect-principal facade and appeared more relaxed than Cody had ever seen her. This caught Cody off guard, and she stepped back, stumbling and falling onto the office couch. Ms. Bixley kept walking forward until she was standing right over Cody.

"It's all right to be scared about what's happening. You should be scared. Every last *one* of you." Ms. Bixley kept staring at her calmly. "Now get the hell out of my office."

=

"We're in trouble, James," Cody said as they left school together. She had filled him in on her chilling encounter with Ms. Bixley, and since neither felt inclined to participate in their respective extracurricular activities, they were leaving early to hit up their favorite diner. "The green light has been given to mess with us. And people seem pretty happy about it."

"I think they're just testing us," James said. "They're provoking us, and we're failing."

"We should let them do whatever they want? Come on, we have to stand up for ourselves."

"The bricks, the ID cards, the demotions—it sucks, I'm with you. But what good does getting angry do? You almost died last night. And now you've got Bixley gunning for you. Fighting back has only made things worse."

"So we shouldn't even react?"

"That's not what I'm saying. Just . . . react better. If they want to be violent, we can be peaceful. If they act petty, we stay classy. We do that, and this will all blow over soon enough."

"All right, Gandhi," Cody said. She was annoyed by how preachy James sounded, but she saw his point.

"Next time one of these idiots acts out, promise me you won't lose your cool?" he said.

"Fine," she said begrudgingly.

"Well, that doesn't inspire much confidence."

"I don't have to like it, okay? But you're right. They want us to overreact so they can justify doing something worse. I won't give them a reason, I promise."

James put his arm around her and kissed her temple, and then they walked up the steps to the Starlite, the local diner. It wasn't busy, so they took seats at the empty counter. A waitress trudged over, weary but smiling.

"Hi, Mom," Cody said.

Her mother, Joanne, reached out and squeezed Cody's arm. "Hi, kids," she said. Joanne was a small woman, her straw-colored hair half gray now after thirty years of working at this same counter. She was an eternal optimist, though, and was proud that her daughter wasn't going to be pouring coffee for a living.

"The usual, please," Cody said.

"Not so fast. What the hell happened last night? I saw the window."

"Sorry, I thought James would get mad at me if I told you," Cody said.

"What?" he said, surprised. Cody kicked his leg under the counter.

"He and his friends were in some stupid water-balloon fight all day, you know, like a prank war. They followed us back to our place and tried to hit us as we ran inside."

"A water balloon shattered your window?" Joanne asked, dubious.

"Yes. It must have been a big one," Cody said. She kicked James again, harder this time.

"Yup. A really big one," he said.

"Wow. Are you all right?"

"We're fine," Cody said.

"And don't worry about replacing the glass—I already made my friend pay for it," James said, and stood up to pull his wallet out of his khakis. He counted out some bills and handed them to Joanne. "Sorry about all that." James sat back down sheepishly, but Cody was the one feeling terrible. She felt bad taking James's money, but she knew he had it and she didn't.

Joanne took the bills, still a bit confused. "Well, thank you. I'd yell at you to be careful playing with water balloons, but that just seems crazy," she said. "Fries and shakes, coming right up."

As her mom walked off to the kitchen, Cody turned to James, ready to apologize, but he was sliding out of his seat. "Be right back," he said, gesturing toward the restrooms. "Can you order a bag of ice for my shin?" James said, smiling as he faked a limp.

"Thank you. I'm sorry about that. My mom has seemed pretty freaked out lately. She doesn't need to know bricks are flying through my window."

"Water balloons, though?" James said, shaking his head. "Not your best work."

Cody laughed as he walked away. She leaned back in her chair, trying to enjoy a rare moment of calm, when a stranger slid into the seat next to her. Pretty rude, she thought, considering the diner was empty. Then the person turned and looked her straight in the eyes.

"It's Cody, right?" he said. He was only a couple of years older than she was but gave off an air of confidence and maturity, as if he had dealt with things that Cody couldn't even fathom. And even as he made the most intense eye contact that Cody had ever experienced, he still managed to keep glancing quickly all around the diner, alert to every corner.

"Do I know you?" she asked. No, obviously. Cody surely would have remembered someone so striking, with his sharp features, tawny skin, and closely cropped dark hair. Even though he seemed to be hiding in a dark hooded sweatshirt and baggy cargo pants, his body appeared to be made up of tightly coiled wires. Whoever this person was, he looked like he had parachuted in straight from an army-recruitment commercial.

"No. But we know you," he said. "We heard you were attacked last night. And we heard how you reacted."

"What do you mean, *we*? And how do you know that?"

"I can't get into it here, but I'll fill you in later." He handed her a slip of paper. "Come to that address tonight. We're having a meeting, and you should be there."

Was this guy serious? He was acting as if the greasy-spoon diner in Shasta was teeming with spies. "Dude, I have no idea what you're talking about," she said.

"The Ones, Cody. We've decided to do something."

Cody felt a chill go down her spine as it dawned on her what this meant. There were others out there, others like her who saw what was coming and realized they had to act. Cody felt vindicated. She wasn't crazy, and she wasn't alone. But even with that thrill, she remembered what she had just promised James. She would stop acting so recklessly, stop making things worse. He was probably right—every rash action of hers had only made people hate them more. Surely whatever group this guy belonged to was doing that to an even greater extreme. Cody took the paper and looked down at the address, but she knew she shouldn't go.

"No, thank you," she said.

He stared at her with piercing dark brown eyes and then reached out and grabbed her arm, his firm grip keeping her whole body in place. Cody knew she had every right to knock him away, to shout for help, to have her mom kick him out, but the power of his look stopped her. Cody saw a kindred spirit, someone equally as passionate and tempestuous as she was, but with a measure of self-possession that she had never been able to manage. She was shocked that such a balance could exist, that a person could radiate so much energy while staying perfectly calm. Even if she didn't go to the meeting, she wanted to learn how that was possible.

"Who are you? What's your name?" she asked.

"Kai," he said softly after looking over his shoulder. "So you'll come, then?"

She wanted to trust him, was practically willing to jump out of her seat and follow him out the door to hop on the back of whatever motorcycle he surely rode in on. But she thought of James, the amazing boy she loved, who had saved her life, who knew her better than anyone, who was always trying to protect her, who had the dimples and the curls, and who was probably walking back to her this very second. She couldn't do that to James.

"No. I can't."

Kai's eyebrows furrowed. "I didn't want to explain this here," he said, frustrated, "but you deserve to know."

He stood up and leaned into Cody's ear, their cheeks practically touching, tiny bits of electricity tickling her nerves. His tone was cold, but his breath on the back of her neck was warm. "As we speak, the government is working on a program that they think will solve the equality problem. They're developing a technology to reverse the genetic engineering of all the existing Ones."

Kai paused.

"They're calling it the Vaccine."

CHAPTER 4

AS JAMES DROVE Cody home from the diner, she sat quietly in the passenger seat, staring out the window in a daze. James couldn't figure out what was bothering her, but he knew from experience that he should probably be apologizing for something. It was never the small stuff that got James in trouble, like not holding open a door or forgetting that she hated cinnamon. In that sense, Cody was super chill. But if it was a mistake like not sticking up for her in front of his parents or disagreeing about something she thought was obvious, then look out, Cody was a pit bull. So as he drove along with the tension thick in the car, James racked his brain for something she could be mad about.

"I'm sorry I gave your mom the money," he said, knowing Cody would probably resent him for paying his way out of trouble. "Your ridiculous story kind of backed me into a corner."

"Yup."

"What does that mean?" he said.

James looked at her and realized she hadn't been listening. "Hey. What's going on?"

"Nothing, I'm sorry. Just spaced out for a second," she said.

"Cody . . ."

He turned to her and saw that she was definitely not spaced out. He could tell by the tiny, tensed muscle in her jaw that her mind was working overtime.

"What do you think you'd be like if you hadn't been genetically engineered?" she finally asked.

"What do you mean?"

"Like, who would you be right now if the scientists hadn't messed around with your DNA? Would you still be the same person?"

James thought for a moment. It was a question he'd considered before, and the answer was obvious to him. Of course he'd be different. He'd look different, his body and mind would work differently, and every experience he'd ever had might have played out differently. Hell, if a butterfly had sneezed differently on the day his brother died, James probably wouldn't even exist. It was kind of pointless to get worked up over it, he thought.

"No, I wouldn't be the same," he said. "I bet I'd be pretty

similar, but who cares? I wouldn't even know any other way to be."

James saw that Cody wasn't satisfied with this. It was different for her, and he understood why. If Cody hadn't been picked for the pilot program, there was a good chance she wouldn't be similar at all. There were plenty of kids in her neighborhood who were living proof of that, kids who had the odds hopelessly stacked against them by virtue of the block they were born on and the parents who bore them. James knew Cody felt guilty about overcoming this, but again, he thought, what was the point?

People were born with all kinds of advantages and disadvantages. You couldn't control it, so how could you feel bad about it? Nor did it make much sense to be proud of it. James knew he didn't possess any advantages because he was particularly deserving of them. And people born with birth defects, incurable diseases, lifelong handicaps—they didn't deserve that, either. As he saw it, that was the whole point of testing this new technology. Once the science was all figured out, no one would ever be born unlucky again.

James turned to Cody. "Why are you asking this?"

Her thousand-yard stare had returned, and James knew he wasn't going to get a real answer. He had come to accept that they would always feel differently about being Ones, always disagree about how much of it was a gift and how much was a curse. And since he was pulling up to her house now, he wasn't going to push her. He did, however, stop the car with an extra hard jolt to the brakes. Cody slammed back in her seat.

"Easy there," she said, a little surprised.

"Just trying to wake you up. You sure you're okay?"

"Yeah, I'm fine. I think I just caught a food coma," she said, then smiled at him playfully. "If I never come out of it, promise me that you won't waste your life sitting at my bedside. You have to live, James, promise me you'll live!" Cody collapsed on top of him in a poorly acted death scene.

James laughed and tried to hold her up, then grabbed her hands in mock seriousness. "I'll mourn silently for a year . . . then grab the first girl I see and head straight for the diner."

Cody smacked his arm. "You would not!" She got her stuff together and started to get out of the car. "Sorry if I was acting weird. Talk to you later tonight?"

"Of course," James said. Cody leaned in for a quick kiss, then shut the door. As she walked up to her tiny house with the faded paint and lopsided porch, James thought about shouting after her. He wanted to reassure her, to ease her guilt and tell her that if she hadn't been a One, he was sure she'd be exactly the same—just as smart, beautiful, fast, witty, and stubborn. That she'd be an identical and equally perfect version of herself. He wanted to shout it after her, but he didn't. Because James knew it wasn't true.

=

Back at home, James ate dinner with his parents at their regularly scheduled time. Michael was nowhere to be found, which had become common in recent days. James didn't know which way he preferred it. With Michael gone, at least he knew there wouldn't be a fight at the dinner table, but his empty chair seemed to create a tension all on its own. As they ate silently, James thought about how much these family dinners had changed. Before Michael went off to college, meals were loud, raucous affairs. The two brothers would be yelling excitedly about something that happened at a sports practice, Arthur would be trying to stump them with a math brainteaser, and Helen would snap her napkin at the boys as they fought over food and made a mess. Tonight, though, it was so quiet that James could hear his parents chewing.

When they finished eating, James helped clear the table, dutifully loaded the dishwasher, and tied up the full trash bag. Then he stepped out of the kitchen door and walked down to drop the trash at the curb. At the bottom of the long driveway, James stopped suddenly. In the darkness just ahead of him, he saw a figure sitting at the edge of the street. After a moment of surprise, James recognized the slumped silhouette of his brother. James crossed behind him and tossed the bag in a garbage can. It rattled loudly, but Michael didn't even look up. James was offended that his brother had ignored him, so he sat down right next to him on the curb.

They sat in silence for a minute, and then Michael reached over to a half-finished six-pack and offered it to James. "Beer?"

"No, thanks," James said.

"Right, stupid question. Of course the perfect son wouldn't have a beer," Michael said.

"What's that supposed to mean?" James asked.

"Look at you. Doing all the chores, getting good grades, captain of the debate team. What an impressive specimen!"

James looked at Michael warily, realizing how drunk he was. He didn't want to fight him and had no interest in provoking him, so he grabbed the beer and popped the top. "Happy?" he asked. "And, by the way, you did all those things, too—pretty well, if I remember correctly."

"No, brother, you do it better than I did. That's the difference," Michael said.

James shook his head, knowing it was pointless to argue. Michael had been his idol for as long as he could remember. James grew up following him around and copying his every move, from the stupid way they still tied their shoes to the part in their hair. If Michael was criticizing

James, then he was really being critical of himself. So James just ignored him and took a swig of beer.

"So you agree, then? You do all that stuff better than me?" Michael asked.

"Shut up, will you?"

"You're better than me, James. It's okay to admit it. Not every person is equal."

"Can we just sit here and enjoy—"

"Say it!" Michael shouted. "Admit that you're better than I am."

"Better at holding my liquor," James said, trying to keep things light.

"Better at everything," Michael said. "Well, almost everything. I bet you still can't get out of a super-deluxe head clamp."

Before James could react, Michael had pounced on him, reached around his neck and under one armpit, and locked his head into a painful position that James was all too familiar with. It was Michael's favorite little-brother torture device, a trump card that could put a stop to any fight. James was always helpless in the grasp of his stronger brother and would eventually concede the point rather than getting choked out. And now he was back in that excruciating position, with the full weight of his brother pushing down on him and the sound of laughter ringing in his ear.

"Still got it, bro!" Michael yelled. "Damn, that was quick."

James felt the searing pain start in his neck and tried to squirm free. But he knew it was hopeless. "All right, you got me. Now let go," he croaked.

But Michael kept leaning down on him, laughing joyfully. "Come on, buddy, you can get out of this, right?"

James began to struggle for real, getting angry now. "Loosen up, I'm serious," he said, starting to get scared. Besides being drunk, his brother had been acting different for a while. This didn't feel like roughhousing. It just felt like James couldn't breathe.

"I know you can get out of this, Superboy," Michael said, even as he tightened his hold. "Or did Mom and Dad not order this skill from the breeding catalog?"

The anger burst out of James in an instant of pure fury. First there was the surge of strength as he twisted his body to grab Michael behind the knees and lift him off his feet. Then he threw both of them to the ground, landing with a crushing thud as he drove his shoulder into his brother's chest. And then, as Michael rolled on top of him, James threw a violent right hook with such power and precision that it shattered his brother's nose with a crunch. James cocked his left arm, ready to throw again, but Michael had collapsed onto his back, blood streaming from his face.

James staggered a few steps away, catching his breath as his heart raced. He tried to process an odd combination of feelings—the thrill of victory mixed with remorse at having hurt a member of his family. But most of all, there was the sensation of something totally new: He had never beaten his brother before, in anything. And now he stood over him, looking down as Michael lifted an arm to gingerly touch his face and then let out a pained moan. James looked on for a moment as tears that he couldn't quite explain began to fill his eyes. Then he turned and walked away.

=

Cody didn't answer her phone as James walked toward her house, so he wasn't too alarmed when her mother opened the door with a look of surprise. Joanne craned her neck to see behind him, worry creeping across her face.

"Is Cody all right?" she asked.

"What?" James said, confused.

"Where is she? Did something happen?"

"I was just coming over to see her . . . is she not here?"

Now full-fledged panic came over Joanne. "She took her bike and said she was going out to meet you."

Inside the house, they tried to call her again, looked around her room, and only after it was clear that Cody was totally off the grid did Joanne think to tell James about the guy at the diner. As she recounted what she saw, James couldn't help but imagine the worst. A stranger had approached her at the counter, whispered to her, left her shaking, and disappeared as quickly as he arrived. Well, that explained Cody's weird behavior on the car ride home. What did this guy say to her? Joanne didn't know much— she was across the diner when they were talking—but somehow saw fit to mention that the guy looked like an underwear model. *Terrific*, James thought, *the one thing we know about Cody's kidnapper is that he's handsome.* Growing more worried, James opened up Cody's computer. He typed in her password and immediately saw the last thing Cody had been looking at: a map and directions to an address outside town.

Within a minute, James was on the road, gunning Joanne's car out of Shasta and toward wherever Cody had been lured. Even as he was desperate to find her, James couldn't help but be angry with her, too. She was always running straight into trouble, and every reckless decision put her in a new, unpredictable bind. James had no idea what this current one would be, but he had a terrible feeling about it. Joanne's car was a piece of junk, and even while stomping down on the accelerator, he felt like he was barely moving.

Miles later, when James saw that he was getting close to the address that he'd written down, he began to recognize his surroundings. He was near Cal State–Redding, the university where his father worked. But instead of taking him onto the familiar campus, the directions led him to an area he'd never been before, which was run-down and seemingly deserted. He stopped the car near a crumbling church and double-checked the address. This was it. James got out of the car and walked up to the entrance of the church. The front doors were padlocked, but he could see some light coming from the windows just above the basement. James walked around to the back of the building and found a rusted metal door that was cracked open.

James stood frozen outside the church, and as he felt a cold sweat start to cover his skin, he wondered if he was about to break his own rule. Wasn't walking blindly through this doorway just as foolish as anything Cody had done? Perhaps, he rationalized, but at least he had a legitimate reason. Cody was in trouble; he was sure of that much. And she wasn't very good at getting out of it on her own.

He pulled the door open and grimaced at the grating screech of its hinges. There was a staircase directly in front of him, dropping down into pitch darkness. He started to walk down, the metal stairs echoing with every step, and reached a dank hallway that had a single lightbulb hanging in it. Then he saw the girl, seated in front of a doorway, staring at him.

James froze and tried to conceal the fear pulsing through him. After a second, though, he relaxed just a bit. All things considered, he realized, his descent into this abyss could have yielded a lot worse. Instead, there was a girl, maybe a couple of years older than him, sitting in a chair. She didn't look very nice—that much was true—but she didn't look like a serial killer, either. Serial killers didn't usually have cute pixie cuts that swooped down over big brown eyes like that. At least that was what James was counting on.

"Hi," he said.

She didn't answer, so he began to walk cautiously toward her. James started to see her more clearly now, struck by the extreme contrast of her jet-black hair against her fair complexion. And she had a few piercings on her face that he didn't even think were possible. When James got halfway down the hallway, she held up her hand to stop him.

"What do you want?" she said.

James didn't really know how to answer that. "I'm here to meet my girlfriend."

"Did she tell you to come here?" the girl asked, eyeing him suspiciously.

"Well . . . yeah. She did."

"All right," she said. "Then tell me which way the wind blows."

"Huh?" James said, not even meaning to speak. Had he heard her correctly? Because if so, he had no idea what she was talking about. And as she stared at him, waiting for an answer, it didn't seem like she was going to repeat the question. "I don't understand. I'm just going to go in there and get my girlfriend, okay?" James took a step forward, but the way the girl stood up from her chair made him stop in his tracks.

"Get the hell out of here," she said, and if she had merely seemed cold and grumpy before, her tone now was downright chilling. James saw the change in her face, the new angles of her nostrils and the flush of her cheek—whatever the "or else" was that she had only implied, James wasn't interested in finding out. So he backed toward the staircase, climbed up to the backyard of the church, and shut the door behind him.

As he stood there trying to figure out what to do next, a cool breeze rustled the branches of a tree above him. Should he go back down there and make up something about the wind? No, he didn't want to do that—it would only make him look stupider. He would be grateful to never encounter that girl for the rest of his life.

James knew Cody was somewhere in the basement of that church, but he still didn't know if she was actually in danger. As he walked back to the street, he looked helplessly at the small illuminated windows that rested just above the ground. Something was happening down there, but the glass was clouded over and he couldn't see inside. Maybe he could slip in through the front doors and find a different way downstairs. Granted, they were locked, but they seemed a lot easier to get past than that girl.

Then, as he made his way back to the front, he noticed a metal grate set against the foundation of the church. He walked over and saw that it was covering some ancient heating equipment with plenty of room in the window well for a person to squeeze in on either side of it. And best of all, James saw on the boarded-up window down there that the wood had half-crumbled off already. He knelt down next to the grate and tried to pry it up with his fingers. It didn't move easily, but he could tell it was just grass and mud holding it down. He pulled harder, got the grate in the air, and gently leaned it against the church, taking care to be as silent as possible. Then he lowered himself into the well, landing softly on the gravel bottom. He turned his attention to the boarded-up window and found a crack that was almost big enough to see through. He could tell there were people on the other side and could hear voices now. If he could just shift it open a little more, he'd have a clear view of what was going on.

But just as James was about to peer inside, he heard the gravel crunch behind him. Before he could turn around, his face was pinned against the concrete wall of the church basement.

"I told you to leave."

It was the same voice that James had heard in the hallway. He twisted his neck just enough to see out of the corner of his eye. The girl was standing behind him with a gun pointed at his head.

CHAPTER 5

CODY HAD SPENT most of the meeting trying not to draw any attention to herself. Between not knowing exactly what was going on and seeing that everyone else was a few years older than her, it seemed wise to find a seat in the back and keep her head down. When she had arrived at the church earlier, she found Kai outside, and he greeted her warmly and led her downstairs. But as other people filed into the large storage room, Kai took a seat up front and left Cody to fill in the blanks herself.

It was pretty obvious that everyone in the room was a One. There were maybe two dozen of them, and Cody realized she had never been in one place with so many Ones before. The thought thrilled her as she contemplated the talent and potential that was gathered in this grimy church basement. At the same time, she had the unfamiliar feeling of being intimidated. It wasn't just that they were older; they also had a confidence and seriousness that she envied. It was the same feeling Kai gave off in the diner, that mix of passion and self-control that Cody found so difficult to balance in her own life.

So Cody sat in the back and listened. A well-dressed, preppy guy named Brandon stood up and began to speak.

"Welcome to the Northern California chapter of the New Weathermen," he said. "I know many of us have been talking in smaller groups, but it's time we get more organized."

"Fuck Amber Reed!" a wild-haired kid shouted from the back.

"Indeed," Brandon said, trying to continue. "But let's not get distracted with the Supreme Court. We can't fix that. It's all these new local laws that are really the problem. And now Congress is writing a new bill they are calling the Equality Act. It's going to make it legal everywhere to discriminate against us for the sake of national security."

Daphne, a girl in the front who looked like an Olympic swimmer, stood up. "People are already starting to get hurt. They found a One in Arizona hanging from a tree last night. He was only fifteen." Daphne wiped tears from her eyes.

"Suicide, they said," someone else mumbled in disgust.

"Interesting call, since the victim had cuts and bruises all over his face."

Cody stiffened up imagining this: a boy, all of fifteen years old, hanging by his neck. She thought about how many people must have had the opportunity to stop it, but not a single one did. Rage began to bubble up inside her.

"An eye for an eye—let's hang one of *them*!" the loudmouth from the back shouted. As everyone yelled at him to calm down, they all called him J-Dog, Cody wondered how his obvious over-aggression had slipped past the genetic engineers.

Brandon tried to get back on track. "Before we do anything, we need to figure out a leadership structure. We need a public relations strategy. We need to figure out how we are going to communicate with the other chapters."

A geeky guy named Marcus jumped in quickly. "I can build a secure server to send messages—"

Daphne interrupted him. "How is this going to stop the next lynch mob?"

A few of the other Ones yelled in agreement. Cody sided with this faction, and she wanted them to go even further. If Kai had been telling the truth about the Vaccine, what were they going to do about *that*? She could barely get her mind around such an absurd idea—technology that could somehow alter your genetic makeup even though you were already a fully formed person. It seemed impossible, but so did a lot of things, including her own perfect genetics.

Cody squirmed in her chair as the debate continued, everyone talking over each other about logistics and how the group would function. They all had a lot of passion, but there was no cohesive plan. It seemed the only thing they agreed on was calling themselves the New Weathermen.

Cody leaned over and tapped Marcus on the shoulder. With his dorky glasses and ill-fitting shirt, he seemed like one of the few people there who wouldn't bite her head off. "What does that name even mean?"

Marcus smiled at her with pride. "We know which way the wind blows."

Oh, really helpful, Cody thought. She was getting frustrated, but then she saw Kai stand up. He surveyed the rest of the Ones, stepped to the center of the room, and spoke for the first time.

"Fact number one: The rest of the country has every right and incentive to be afraid of us. Our society is set up as a gigantic zero-sum game. As we start to acquire more resources, both tangible and intangible, there will be less for everyone else. They are going to act rationally and try to prevent this from happening.

"Fact number two: They can, in fact, do just that. They control the government, the financial system, the media, and the military. We, on the other hand, have nothing. No money, no organization, no access to the traditional levers of power. This is going to be the harsh reality for at least the next five to ten years.

"Fact number three: If we don't do something, we are doomed. Inaction is capitulation. So our choice is already made. We must resist, we must fight back, and we must degrade any entity that seeks to force us down. Whether we have a vice-treasurer or an encrypted e-mail network, I don't care. Whether we use pipe bombs or speeches, I don't care. Until total victory or total annihilation, we follow one rule: The New Weathermen protect the basic rights of Ones at any cost."

As Kai returned to his seat, there were loud murmurs of assent. For her part, Cody wanted to jump up, rush over, and hug him. He had articulated exactly what she already knew to be true: A storm was coming, and they had no choice but to face it head-on. And then it dawned on Cody with a wave of excitement—she saw how the wind was blowing.

Before the next person could speak, the back door of the storage room crashed open. As Cody and everyone else turned to look, she let out an audible gasp. James was being led into the room at gunpoint.

Cody covered her mouth, not knowing whether to scream out or hide. A girl Cody had met outside, Taryn, was pushing James to the front of the room.

"I found him outside, spying. Not sure how much he

heard," Taryn said. She turned to Kai. "What are we going to do with him?"

Brandon jumped out of his seat. "Whoa, hold on a second," he shouted. "First of all, why are you asking Kai? No one's in charge here, remember?"

Taryn rolled her eyes, then made a big show of addressing the whole room. "Sorry . . . what are *we* going to do about this?"

"And second of all," Brandon continued, "why the hell do you have a gun? We're certainly not going to kill him!"

"Gimme the gun—I'll kill him!" J-Dog shouted.

Taryn turned to Brandon. "Wake up, dude. This is exactly the type of stuff we need to worry about now," she said. "If you want me in charge of security, then don't bitch about how I handle it."

Cody watched as Kai stepped in between them and lightly pressed on Taryn's arm to lower the gun. And then Cody made eye contact with James for the first time, saw the panic on his face, and realized she had to do something.

"He's with me!" she shouted from the back of the room. Everyone turned to look at her. "It's fine. He's with me. And he's a One."

"And who the hell are you?" Brandon sneered.

"It's cool, I invited her," Kai said. "She's the high school kid I told you about. The one who fought back."

"Since when are we including kids at these things?" Taryn asked.

"Hey, remember the point of all of this? We're a minority that makes up one percent of the population. . . . We need all the help we can get," Kai said. Then he turned back to Cody. "Do you vouch for him?"

Cody hesitated. She could certainly vouch that James was a terrific person, a good boyfriend, moral, trustworthy, and kind. But somehow she knew that was not what Kai was asking. And now her standing in the group would be forever tied to James. But what else could she do other than vouch for him? She'd just have to make James understand that whether or not he completely agreed with what was happening here, he'd have to accept it. Everyone else in the church saw what the Equality Movement was trying to do—if James didn't, Cody would make him.

She looked Kai in the eye and nodded. She vouched for him.

Up in the front of the room, Kai turned to James and gave him a rough pat on the arm. "Welcome," he said. "Have a seat."

=

After the meeting ended, Cody waited until they had walked away from the church before she turned on James.

"I can't believe you followed me here!" she said.

"Are you serious? Don't you mean *thank you*?"

"Thank you for what? I was fine. Meanwhile, you almost got yourself shot and made us both look like idiots."

"Which all could have been prevented if you had just told me where you were going."

"I wasn't allowed to. Kai told me to come alone."

"Oh. Kai. I didn't realize he was in charge of our relationship."

"He's not. And neither are you. You're not my babysitter."

"Right, I'm sorry. Your mom's freaking out, I'm worried sick, but from now on I'll just wait until it's crystal clear that you're in trouble before I lift a finger to help. Wouldn't want to embarrass you again."

As James walked off ahead of her, Cody realized she was being a jerk. She caught up with him and grabbed his arm.

"You didn't embarrass me, okay? It's just that . . . you heard what they were talking about down there. I didn't want us to look like ignorant kids," she said.

"Yeah, I did hear them. And honestly, they're all crazy."

"James, keep your voice down."

"I'm sorry. But they're talking about a national network of college students that's going to run around—doing what? Planting bombs? Can we just get out of here, please?"

Now something scarier occurred to Cody, an issue that was much bigger than their petty bickering. She was almost afraid to ask, but she had to.

"You actually think we deserve this, don't you?"

"What do you mean?"

"You agree with them, the rest of the country. You think we are a mistake—a problem that needs fixing. That we shouldn't be treated the same as everyone else." Cody glared at him. "Am I right?"

James struggled to formulate a response. "Not exactly, okay? I just . . . I understand why people think it's unfair. We have an advantage, don't we? And if there needs to be some adjustments to make things fair again, I don't believe that bombing government buildings is an appropriate response."

"*Adjustments?* Kids are getting killed! No one should be punished simply because of how they were born. I thought we always agreed on that."

"We do. But whatever is happening in there," James said, pointing back toward the church, "that's not the solution."

Cody's heart sank as she realized how big the rift was between her and James. But she knew this wasn't the moment to convince him. She needed to get him away from the rest of the Ones and explain things in the car. Make him understand that he was now obligated, at the very least, to keep quiet about this. She had vouched for him.

As she pushed James toward her mother's car, she heard Kai call out from behind her. "Cody!" he yelled. "Wait up a second."

Cody and James stopped at the edge of the street, and Kai jogged over to them. He stood between them and put his arms around both their shoulders. Cody thought it was supposed to be friendly, but it still felt a little weird.

"I'm glad you two made it today," Kai said. "I know there may have been a lot to take in, but I hope you felt it was worthwhile."

"Yeah, thanks for including us. We're honored to be part of this," Cody said.

"Okay, great. That's what I expected," Kai said. Then he turned to look at James. Cody fixed her gaze on him as he stood silently for a moment.

"Yup. Ditto," James said.

"Well, listen . . . I think there's a real opportunity to get you guys organized over at the high school. Like I said inside, it can't just be us old geezers—if this is going to work, we need every One to be involved."

"Yeah, I totally agree," Cody said.

"Here, take my number," Kai said, handing her a slip of paper. "We should bounce some ideas around. And don't worry, it's not my regular phone. This one is safe to call."

Cody took the paper and slid it into her pocket. She could feel James staring daggers at her. And yes, they were definitely daggers, not butter knives. Cody wanted to pull Kai aside and ask him about the Vaccine, since that was the whole reason she had come in the first place. But she had a feeling that she should focus on separating Kai and

James as quickly as possible. Nothing good was going to come from their interacting any longer. Anyway, she had Kai's number now—she could ask him about the Vaccine on her own.

"Sounds good," Cody said. "We should really be going now."

"Of course. Be safe, and we'll talk soon," Kai said. He nodded at both of them and then jogged back toward the church.

James started walking to the car. Cody grabbed her bike and ran to catch up with him. She threw it in the trunk and got inside, and then they rode back to Shasta in silence.

It was the last time they'd be together before everything changed.

=

When Cody woke up on the morning of List Day, she had a clear plan in her head. She was going to jog over to James's house, thank him for looking out for her, and then in the calmest way possible explain why she agreed with the New Weathermen. If he disagreed, she'd be disappointed, but at least they'd be communicating about it. And if she absolutely had to, she would tell him the rumor about the Vaccine. That was what had worked on her, after all, when Kai had left her in the diner. She had imagined James or herself being irrevocably changed, and it was too much to bear. She liked them the way they were

and knew James did, too. So that was the plan—
she truly believed that she and James could fix things.

But when James threw open her bedroom door while
Cody was still blinking awake, she knew something terrible had happened.

"Have you checked your computer yet?" he asked
gravely.

"No. I just woke up. What's going on? Why are you over
here so early?"

James picked up Cody's computer. "Here. See for yourself." He handed it to her and gave her some space.

Cody opened the computer and caught up with the
rest of world. At six o'clock that morning, every American
citizen had received the same e-mail. It was sent by a
woman named Edith Vale, an analyst at the National
Security Agency. Attached to the e-mail was a remarkable
document.

It was a list of every single One in the country.

It included their names, addresses, and photos. Each
identity was confirmed by the Social Security number
that the NIH used to monitor the genetic-engineering
program. The List, it seemed, could not be more compre-
hensive and official. It had everyone from the most recent
newborns to those in their early twenties. Cody gasped in
horror, realizing the gravity of this action. The List was
meant to unleash terror. To serve as a map. To expose each

individual One to the fate they deserved. Edith Vale had put a bull's-eye on every single one of them.

And then came the greater shock.

Cody's name wasn't on it.

The List was divided by ZIP code, and Cody quickly scrolled down to the section that contained the citizens of Shasta. She saw James's name. She saw the names of the Ones she knew from school. She saw Kai's name and others that she vaguely recognized. Cody scrolled around, checking in every possible way. She imagined that maybe they had mixed up her name somehow, or where she lived. If this was a list of every single One, then she had to be on it. She did a formal computer search within the entire document, and still there was nothing. No matter how hard she looked, her name wasn't listed.

Cody turned to James, who was hanging over her shoulder searching, as well. They locked eyes as the same thought shook each of them with all the grace of an earthquake.

Cody wasn't a One.

CHAPTER 6

CODY WAS ALWAYS fast, of course. How she had the wherewithal to stand, to move, to dart out of the house, James didn't understand. But once she had the head start, there was no catching her.

James couldn't fathom how anyone could have moved a muscle in the moments after Cody had looked at the List. Just a second earlier, she had seemed paralyzed in front of her computer screen with James frozen behind her, and then, in the doorway to Cody's room, her mother appeared, crying. James watched as the two of them locked eyes, and he saw the momentous but silent exchange. As James accepted his own paralysis, grateful that it gave him time to process all the new bombs that had detonated in his life, Cody bolted. She knocked over her mom, grabbed her sneakers, and burst out the door of the house, and by the time James got his body working and stuck his head outside, she was a speck disappearing at the end of the street.

Ironic, James thought. She wasn't a One, but she was still the fastest person in town. And then he immediately hated himself for thinking it.

With Cody gone and Joanne slumped over crying, James didn't know where to go. To school, he figured. It was still a school day. Or did an unauthorized national-security breach that threatened the lives of hundreds of thousands of children mean that school was canceled, like a snow day? James tried to wrap his mind around exactly what had happened that morning. Some things made perfect sense: The federal government had a database of all the Ones. They were being studied, after all, so of course some organization was keeping track of them. But this woman—Edith Vale—what the hell was she doing? James didn't find it crazy that she had access to the List; he assumed employees at the NSA had access to everything. He knew the Clear Browsing History option on his computer was a joke and behaved accordingly.

Before he went anywhere, James felt like he was supposed to say something to Cody's mom.

"I'm sorry," he said, not fully understanding what he meant. Joanne didn't respond, and James couldn't resist asking a question. He spoke softly, trying not to be rude. "Why did you lie to her?" he asked.

Joanne looked up at him, devastated. "She was never supposed to know. This list . . . why would anyone release it?" she asked.

James considered the question and concluded that this list was meant as a gesture of encouragement. A gift to everyone in the Equality Movement who wanted to get rid of the Ones. Of course, *get rid of* could mean a lot of different things. Some people just wanted to ban the technology, as the Supreme Court had recently ruled. Some people wanted to restrict how the existing Ones could go about their lives. And then there was the last group. James knew how they defined *get rid of.* They were pretty literal-minded, those people. The thought that the List might be a gift to them sent a chill down his spine.

Even with this new bull's-eye on his back, James left Cody's house and drove to school. There was something reassuring about sticking to his normal routine. If the government had turned against him and his girlfriend was a different person, then maybe sitting in good old first-period history class was exactly what he needed. Lots of bygone eras had terrible problems; maybe he could live vicariously through all the awful stuff that happened in the past and ignore what was going on in the present.

By the time James had parked his car and started walking up to school, he had already begun to regret this decision. Immediately, it was clear that everyone milling around outside was staring at him. As James approached the entrance, his friend Andrew from the debate team fell in stride with him.

"Are you crazy? You're the only One who showed up today," Andrew said nervously.

"What am I supposed to do, become a hermit?" James replied, and kept walking toward the door.

"Yeah, exactly. For today at least."

"Andrew, the List has all my information on it. My name, my address, my photo. If someone wants to find me, I can't stop them."

"Well, I think someone does. And you just made it pretty easy."

James followed Andrew's gaze and saw Marco and the rest of his Bench Mob blocking their path. As James slowed down and stopped in front of them, Marco held up a piece of paper. It was a printout of James's info from the List.

"You're famous, buddy. I found you on the Internet," Marco said with his signature half smile.

As usual, Marco's buddies reflexively formed a semi-circle around James. He wasn't on the edge of a cliff this time, but it still wasn't very comfortable.

"Yeah, I guess so. Breaking news, huh?"

Andrew put his hand on James's shoulder. "Come on, you should get out of here. I'll ride home with you."

Marco nodded. "That's actually a good idea. You should probably get going."

James shook loose from Andrew's grasp. "I'm not leaving. I'm going to my history class."

"James, trust me, let's go," Andrew said.

"No."

Marco started laughing and turned to his posse. "Look, guys, they're debating! You two are the best we've got?"

James shrugged him off and began to walk forward. But Marco stopped him with a stiff forearm to his chest. "I'm serious," Marco said, "beat it."

James tried again to walk toward school, but Marco pushed him backward. The first push wasn't that hard, but the second one was. It startled James, and he saw in Marco's eyes that he was serious. He was ready to throw down right in front of the school if James gave him the slightest opening. So James didn't lift a finger, but he kept trying to walk. Another push, harder this time. Marco was strong, and each shove sent James scuffling back through the parking lot.

Finally, after six, seven, eight times, James had enough. He felt the same sensation buzz up into his ears that he'd experienced right before he pummeled his brother. It wasn't as foreign this time, and he knew what it meant—what it could allow him to do. He had hoped to avoid reaching this point, but that willpower left him now. Marco was obviously not going to stop.

After the last push, James took off his backpack and

threw it on the ground. He looked Marco square in the eye.

"If you really want to, fine. Let's do it."

And then, just as James stepped forward to meet Marco face-to-face, a car came speeding into the parking lot, its engine roaring and tires squealing. The car steered right for the crowd that had gathered, forcing people to jump out of the way. And just before it hit anyone, the car screeched to a halt right next to James and Marco.

The passenger's side door swung open. "Get in, you idiot."

James ducked down to look inside. But he already knew what was happening, recognized the car instantly—and the voice as well.

"Now, James!"

It was his brother.

≡

When they had driven long enough in silence, James finally turned to Michael, ready to speak, but he was immediately startled by the grotesque bruising around his brother's nose, a purple-and-green oil stain that was spreading out over half his face. *Oh, great,* James thought, *so where were we?*

Feeling guilty, he took a breath.

"Thanks," James said. "I was fine, but still . . ." He paused for a second. "And I'm sorry about last night."

"I'm just running an errand for Dad. He asked me to get you, and I did."

James nodded. If Michael didn't want to talk, that was fine. The cold shoulder was better than a super-deluxe head clamp.

They rode in silence again for a while, and James could tell they were headed for Arthur's office at the university. He had started down the same road the previous night, before he found Cody and the New Weathermen at the church. James wondered where she had run off to now, grateful at least that she hadn't joined him at school. He knew that he needed to find her soon, that they had a lot to talk about. But for the time being, he could tell he was stuck in protective custody.

Michael shuffled in his seat and rolled the window up. "Look, James, I don't agree with what happened this morning. You know, with the List."

"Really? I thought everyone in the Equality Movement was for universal exposure."

"I'm not part of the Equality Movement," Michael said quickly. James gave him a dubious look. "You know, not officially or anything like that."

"But you agree with them. What's the difference?"

"I agree with the principle of equality—of course I do! Who doesn't?"

"*They* don't!" James shouted. "Putting *equality* in their name is just a gimmick, a marketing tool. The Equality Act is going to pass next week, and it will mean they can just snap their fingers and say I'm an enemy combatant. They can detain me for no reason and strip me of all my rights. Does that sound equal to you?"

"You know what else isn't equal—"

"I know, I know, I KNOW! Me! Me being alive isn't fair, I get it, Michael!"

Michael shrank back as James became crazed. "So what should we do?" James continued. "I don't mean the whole world—what should *you* and *I* do about it? Should I disappear? Should I chop off a leg? Poke out an eye? What can I do so you don't hate me?"

"I don't hate you."

James took a deep breath, taking solace even in such a backhanded compliment.

Michael continued, though. "But I hate what Mom and Dad decided to do after Thomas died."

"Yeah?" James responded. "You and me both."

$$=$$

James and Michael signed in as guests to the science building and found their father in the cramped, cluttered office that was down the hall from his laboratory. The college lab was always buzzing with undergraduate chemistry majors, but Cal State–Redding was particularly known for agricultural engineering. California had a lot of farmland, no water, and avocados, oranges, and tomatoes that were ripe all year—some pretty smart people were making that math work. Arthur had been a professor there for twenty-five years, and he and his team were called the Veggie Whisperers. They could make a piece of produce do whatever they wanted.

When James walked into the office, Arthur jumped to his feet and rushed over to hug him.

"Thank God you're okay. I was already here when I found out what happened. What a despicable act of treason." Arthur turned to Michael. "Thank you for catching up with him."

"So what now? Am I grounded in your office or something?" James asked.

"No. But you're certainly not roaming around by yourself like nothing happened. There are horrible things happening all over the country. So for now, for today, you can hang out here. I'm sorry."

James plopped down on a tiny sofa and sighed. "Well, it's not your fault. At least I can take a nap—"

"It is his fault."

James and his father jerked their heads toward Michael. Did he really just say that?

"Excuse me?" Arthur said.

"Come on, Dad, don't tell me you didn't see this coming. You're too smart for that. Seventeen years ago, you and Mom made a choice. You must have known this was going to happen eventually."

James looked over to his father, waiting for him to explode. He had never heard his brother talk to him like that. Michael wasn't just needling him—he was being downright confrontational.

Instead of flying off the handle, though, Arthur went back to his desk, slumped in his chair, and looked forlornly at the ceiling.

"You're right, Michael. You're absolutely right. I did know this would happen one day. And whatever this thing is that's going on between you two . . . I saw that coming, too. But I made myself blind to it, refused to acknowledge the reality. Your mother and I wanted a child. To keep this family intact. It was that simple. So we made a choice and here we are. People do reckless things when they want something badly enough."

James couldn't believe what he was hearing. He could barely muster the courage to look his father in the eye, but he had to ask. "So you regret it, then?"

Arthur turned to James and held his gaze for a long time. "Of course not. I cherish you, James. But now I see it. If we had it all to do over again—and by we, I mean everyone—we should have never mixed up human beings with this terrible technology."

James's discomfort was turning to anger now, especially because he could see his brother nodding smugly out of the corner of his eye. "Well, you did *mix us up* in it!" he exclaimed. "And I'm here! So are thousands of others! Should we just be locked away somewhere to solve the problem for you?"

"Of course not, James. You're not understanding me—I didn't mean to upset you. You are a beautiful human being, and you deserve to walk around with your head held high. But I do believe there is a way to solve this problem. Before the country burns itself down. There has to be a middle ground, a compromise. I have faith we can figure that out." Arthur paused for a second, then laughed and stood up. "But what do I know . . . I'm just a guy who needs to go check the internal body temperature of some zucchinis."

Arthur gathered some folders and headed for the door. "Michael, do me a favor, stick around with your brother for today at least. We'll figure out the next step when we're all home later."

Michael and James exchanged a frustrated look but didn't push back. Then, before Arthur could leave, there was a loud knock on his door. He opened it to reveal a soldier in full combat gear standing in the hallway. James immediately noticed the size of the assault rifle hanging off his shoulder. It was a pretty startling sight in the middle of his dad's lab.

"Professor Livingston, I need you to sign for this package." The soldier was holding a small cardboard box and a digital clipboard. He tried to hand Arthur the box, but Arthur was startled and shifted his body to block the doorway.

"Not right now, please. I'll get it later," he said.

"Sir, I have strict orders to make this delivery. You are required to accept it and confirm your receipt—"

"All right, all right, I'll sign. Give it to me."

James watched as his father took the box from the soldier, pinned it under his arm, and quickly signed the scanner. Without turning around or saying another word to his boys, he stepped out of his office and walked briskly down the hall. James found the whole exchange utterly bizarre. And before his father rushed away, James had a second to glance at the delivery sticker on the side of the package.

It was sent from the National Institutes of Health.

CHAPTER 7

IT DIDN'T MAKE any sense to Cody. There had to be a mistake.

She wasn't on the list of Ones. The List of Ones came from the government. The government ran the program. There was no record of her being part of the genetic-engineering pilot program. And yet . . .

Cody couldn't admit what this might mean. Not yet; it was too much to think about. That was why she had run out of the house, sprinted down the street, and ducked into Shasta's foothills. She kept going higher and higher, like she always did with James, but this time she didn't head for their usual spot. She needed to be alone, so she slalomed through the pine trees, charting an unknown course. The harder she ran, the easier it was to stop her mind from racing. So she ran until exhaustion, but eventually there was no farther to go. She was at the top of a bluff, chest heaving, tears coming, brain starting to function again. And now she couldn't escape from it. She had to acknowledge it was true.

Cody was simply born this way.

There was no fancy science behind it. No lucky lottery win. No grocery shopping for the right genes. No special advantage, no predetermined path to intelligence and beauty and fitness. Everything that Cody had attributed to being a One was just her regular old self. Even as her entire identity and all her relationships were thrown out of balance, Cody couldn't suppress a powerful feeling that was leaping from every cell of her body: pride.

When she kicked everyone's ass in a cross-country meet—that was her. When she got straight As—her. When she caused a fender bender crossing the street because a gust of wind blew at her skirt—too much of her.

But as validating as this was to realize, Cody now also had to admit that her entire life had been a lie. Ever since she could walk and talk, she had always been told she was a One. So that was how she behaved. That was what informed everything she did. That was how she interacted with everyone she met.

And that was how she fell for James.

Besides all the superficial reasons, they were drawn to each other because they shared an uncommon bond.

A different perspective on the world and also a responsibility that they both took very seriously. A responsibility to pay the world back for their good fortune. Cody knew she would be a doctor; James knew he would go into politics. And then, as the events of the past few months put them on an emotional roller coaster, they had grown even closer as pillars of support. The foundation of that relationship was now a lie, and Cody didn't know what that meant for them.

Her feelings toward her mother were even harder to pin down. Anger, disappointment, confusion . . . and maybe sympathy? No, Cody couldn't forgive her—not yet, at least. She had lied to Cody every day for sixteen years. She had deprived Cody of growing up as her true self. She had run her own little science experiment without any regard for how it might end.

Now Cody understood the weird way her mom had been looking at her recently. It wasn't fear of losing her, not separation anxiety based on Cody's preparing to leave Shasta behind. It was regret about what she had orchestrated, hindsight that the seemingly brilliant gift to her daughter was turning into a curse. And there was no solution, because she could never tell Cody the truth. So she had to watch her daughter suffer, get harassed, fear for her life. Somehow, to admit the lie would have been worse. They had come too far for that.

But the List was out now. A stranger named Edith Vale

had decided for them. Cody knew she had to descend from this hilltop and find her mom. They needed to have the first honest talk of her life.

When Cody walked back into her house, it was dead quiet, and the front door was still open. She had half expected to find her mom and James waiting breathlessly by the door, but apparently people didn't do that for hours on end. She walked through the house and found Joanne sitting on the floor in Cody's room, a photo album open on her lap.

Joanne looked up in relief as Cody entered. "Hi, sweetie. Are you okay?"

"So it's really true? I'm not . . ."

Joanne shook her head, tears falling from her eyes. For Cody, though, the anger built back up again.

"Why did you lie to me?"

"Cody, I'm sorry."

"What else isn't true? Am I adopted? Is this even my real name?"

"Everything else is real, sweetheart, I promise you."

"Then why? You didn't believe I could turn out like this on my own?"

"Of course that's not—"

"You give birth to this sweet baby girl and then thought so little of her that you had to invent a lie for her to turn out all right?

"No—"

"You thought that without lying, I'd somehow grow up to be—"

"Like me! A nobody! That's what I thought, Cody! I thought you deserved a better chance than I had. So that you wouldn't grow up to be a single mother working at the same diner since she was fifteen. I wanted something better for you. Is that so bad?"

"Mom . . ."

"How else was I going to give you that chance? I was a stupid eighteen-year-old who was lonely after a shift one night. There was a guy at the counter with a nice smile and a shiny new truck. It was the first week of spring. I barely blinked, and then I was holding you in my arms. Look at me, Cody. Look at our house, our block, our neighborhood. What else did I possibly have to give you? Nothing. *Nothing.* So I told you a story when you were little. And then I kept that story alive, and wouldn't you know it, it was like it went straight from my lips to God's ears. I mean, look at you! It worked, Cody. I swear, it was working like a dream. The way you acted in school, the way you played with the other kids, it was like you had a ray of sunlight shining off your eyes at all times. Everyone else believed it—of course they did—it was obvious you were special! And then, when you were old enough to really understand, I stuck to that story. The way you accepted it and embraced it and took responsibility for it . . . it was remarkable, sweetie. You are an incredible young woman, and I couldn't be prouder."

Cody tried to put herself in her mother's shoes. She saw how all this had happened and understood that once it had started, it was never supposed to unravel like this. And she saw her mother's intentions. Like everything else Joanne had ever done, she had been looking out for her daughter.

"I get it, Mom. I don't hate you, okay? But I don't know if I can forgive you."

"Why not?"

"Because I'll never know for sure now—whether this is who I really am, or if I just turned out this way because of some trick. You took that away from me."

"Cody, I watched it happen—this is who you really are."

Cody could only shrug. Maybe her mom was right, but it was pointless to argue. She'd never know; there was no way to start her life from scratch and see how it would have unfolded. On a day that she had discovered so much about who she was, it somehow felt like she'd lost out on something much greater.

=

Cody spent the rest of the night alone in her room. She wanted to see James and figure out what this meant for them, but the conversation with her mother had left her spent. She couldn't have an equally heavy talk with James right now. Her attention drifted down to the floor, where the photo albums that her mom had taken out were still lying open. Cody paged through them, feeling like she was looking at her life for the first time.

The pictures told a heartwarming story: a little girl and her mother, alone but for each other, *Us-against-the-world* practically written on their faces. Cody thought about what her mother had said earlier, how Joanne had nothing to give to her daughter. That was not what came across in the photographs. Sure, the birthday parties weren't fancy and the Halloween costumes were thrown together from the closet, but the girl in the photos didn't seem to notice any of that. She was healthy and happy. Cody considered what her mom had done to make that happen. *A lot*. Worked her ass off. Sacrificed her personal life. Put every extra dollar into something that Cody wanted, even if it was some junky magnifying glass from the thrift store. *She gave me everything*, Cody thought. Why couldn't her mom have had faith that that would have been enough? Why did she also have to lie?

Cody went to bed still torn about what she had discovered that day. She realized it was all about perspective. If she looked backward, she grew angry and frustrated, pissed off that she had never really been in control of her life. If she considered the future, that new feeling of pride and possibility swelled up in her again. But she didn't live in the past and she didn't live in the future, she was stuck agonizingly in the present. And at the moment, that wasn't a very comfortable place to be.

So she tossed and turned for a long time, feeling like she'd never get to sleep. But she must have drifted off at some point. That was the only way to explain how she woke up suddenly with a firm hand pressed against her mouth.

Cody tried to sit up and wriggle out of her bed, but a strong arm held her down. It was dark in her room, and she couldn't tell who was on top of her. As her panic grew into sheer terror, she heard someone softly make a sound.

"Shhhhhhhh . . ."

Yeah, she was already quiet, but as soon as the hand moved from her mouth, she was going to wake up the entire West Coast.

"Promise me you'll be quiet, Cody. It's Kai."

Kai? What the hell was Kai doing in her room pinning her down to the bed? And was that terrifying or a relief? She was flooded with embarrassment as she thought about her messy room, her tangled hair, and her thin shirt.

Cody nodded her head, and Kai removed his hand. Her eyes began to adjust, and she made out the razor-sharp cheekbones under his dark hood. Kai knelt down next to her bed and started to whisper.

"I'm sorry to scare you, but this can't wait." He stared into her eyes, and for a second, Cody forgot to be scared.

"What are you doing here? And how did you even get in?" she asked.

"Cody, please keep your voice down. Your mom is right down the hall."

"Kai, what is going on?" Cody whispered loudly.

"We need to talk. I can't imagine you're surprised to hear that. You came to our meeting, we trusted you, and now you've made us look very foolish."

"What do you mean?"

Even in the dark, Cody could feel Kai looking at her like she was crazy. "Cody, you're not on the List. You're not a One. You lied to us."

Cody had never felt stupider. In all her soul-searching about what it meant to not be a One, she had never considered that it also made her a liar. Not intentionally, of course, but that was beside the point. And if anyone might get pissed about a person lying about being a One, it would probably be the New Weathermen. This nighttime visit suddenly made a lot of sense.

"I'm sorry, I didn't know, either. I swear, I can explain—"

Kai put a finger against her lips to stop her from getting too loud. His touch was warmer than she'd expected.

"Let's talk about this outside—we need to figure out what to do. We're out back—come meet us," Kai whispered, and then stood up.

"Us?" Cody asked.

"Just come outside."

Kai slipped out of her room as silently as he must have entered, and Cody was left in bed, suddenly shivering. The

New Weathermen were demanding to see her in the dead of night. They thought she was a liar. This could be a pleasant nighttime stroll, or it could end with her in the trunk of a car.

Cody knew she didn't have much of a choice, so she threw on a sweatshirt and shoes and slipped quietly out the back door. At the back edge of her yard, she glimpsed two figures waiting in the shadows.

Kai, with his deep eyes reflecting the moonlight.

And Taryn. The girl who casually carried around a gun.

"Thanks, Cody. We just need to talk," Kai said.

"I promise I didn't mean to lie the other day," Cody started.

Taryn cut her off. "The New Weathermen have a strict policy about spies infiltrating our group."

"I'm not a spy! I honestly thought I was a One!" Cody quickly explained everything she had just learned from her mother. Even if it all made sense, she knew it sounded a little convenient.

Kai and Taryn looked at each other, weighing how much they believed. Taryn shook her head. "The rules exist for a reason. Even if there's a chance she's telling the truth, we can't risk it," she said.

Kai was silent for a moment. He stared long and hard at Cody, and her skin started to prickle from his intensity. "I believe her."

"That's great, but it doesn't matter," Taryn responded.

"If she walked down to the police station tomorrow and told them what she heard, we'd all be screwed. They'd have us locked up in two minutes. All of us."

"I am not going to do that," Cody said.

"But how do we know that, Cody?" Kai asked. "I need to be able to convince everyone else that there's no chance of that happening."

"Because I still agree with you guys!" Cody shouted.

Taryn looked at her quizzically. "You do?"

Cody nodded. She hadn't given it much thought yet, but she instinctively knew it was what she really believed. Her biography had changed, but her principles were the same as ever. "Yes. I'm still on your side. I still believe Ones are being persecuted unfairly. And I still believe that the only way to fix it is to fight back." She thought back to what Kai had said at the meeting and looked him in the eye. "We follow one rule: Protect our rights at all costs." And then Cody caught herself. "*Your* rights," she added sheepishly.

Cody noticed that Kai was trying to suppress a proud smile. Taryn saw it, too, and rolled her eyes, clearly irritated.

"I'm glad you feel that way. We need all the help we can get," Kai said.

"So you're not going to kill me?"

"No, I guess not. And *I* was never going to kill you," Kai said, and then nodded at Taryn. "She was."

Cody glanced over at Taryn and didn't feel much relief. If looks could kill, Cody was already a chalk outline.

"How?" Cody asked, unable to help herself.

Taryn seemed to relish giving an answer. "Put it this way: You wouldn't even know that it happened."

Cody tried not to gulp. "Okay, then. Well, thanks for coming by and clearing this up, I guess," she said, then turned to Kai. "So does this mean I'm officially a Weatherman?"

Kai shook his head and laughed. "No, not even close." And then he looked at Cody with those piercing eyes and turned dead serious.

"You're going to need to prove yourself first."

CHAPTER 8

WHEN JAMES WOKE up on List Day plus 1, the atmosphere of hysteria still hung in the air like a stubborn layer of smog. As of yet there was no nationwide purge of the Ones who were exposed by the List, but stories of targeted violence drifted in from around the country. Most of them started in a similar manner to James's experience in the school parking lot but didn't end with a big brother riding in to the rescue. Members of the Equality Movement felt as if they had tacit approval from the government to go after Ones now. Why else would someone from a federal agency have released the List? Sure, various political leaders made broad statements that condemned violence, but on the Internet, Edith Vale was being hailed as a hero, a whistle-blower of the best kind, someone who shone a light on a problem that the majority of the country wanted to expose. The attitude of most of the country could be seen in the fresh graffiti that was popping up everywhere: the ubiquitous equal signs, of course, but there was also a new word finding its way onto brick walls and abandoned trucks—*gennycide*.

Scanning through all the stories online, James saw reports of resistance, too. The headlines were pretty intense: EMPTY SCHOOL BUS EXPLODES IN THE BRONX . . . CONGRESSWOMAN'S HOME BURNS DOWN, ARSON SUSPECTED . . . ATLANTA POLICE DEPARTMENT CRIPPLED BY CYBERATTACK. It was clear to James that pockets of New Weathermen were starting to lash out, and he shook his head with disappointment as he read the stories. The extremists on both sides were digging in.

Despite all this, James had negotiated an uneasy compromise with his parents that allowed him to leave the house just to go to school. The last thing he wanted was to be cooped up with Michael hovering over him, so he argued that going about his normal life was the best statement he could make right now. If he didn't, then the terrorists would win—the terrorists in this case being his own government and most of his fellow citizens. Maybe that was a little melodramatic, but the point still stood: James didn't want to get bullied into disappearing from society. His parents understood that and finally allowed him to leave the house without his brother as an escort.

And James's house wasn't exactly the most comfortable place to hang around now. Since the List had come out, his brother had berated his father for choosing to have James, and his father had basically admitted it was a terrible mistake. James actually felt a measure of relief that some of the uncomfortable dynamics he could never put his finger on were finally coming to light. That nagging sense that he could never be perfect enough made sense now. No report card was ever going to fix a "mistake."

Making things worse, his parents had also seen that Cody wasn't on the List, and James's mom couldn't bite her tongue as she handed him a plate of toast that morning.

"I always had a feeling about that girl," she said with a note of pride.

James glared at her and walked out of the kitchen. He felt desperate to get away from these people. Luckily for him, his address had been circulated to everyone alive who might want to harm him, so getting out of the house actually made sense.

James texted Cody and arranged to pick her up on the way to school. When he pulled up in front of her house, a weird sensation of butterflies swarmed his stomach. It was the same feeling he'd experienced when he arrived to take Cody on their first date more than a year ago, and it grew even more intense when she had walked out of the house and James saw her wearing a dress for the first time. Today, though, James wasn't so much nervous as confused. Cody—the epitome of being a One and his equal in all ways—somehow wasn't that person anymore. But that made no sense, because Cody was obviously still the same person. At least James hoped she was.

When she bounded out the door and loped down to his car, James's fears melted away. He pushed open the passenger's side door for her, but Cody circled around the Jeep and leaned into James's window to plant a kiss on his lips. They held together for a moment, sharing all the wild emotions of the past day.

Cody finally pulled back as James reached up to tuck a strand of hair behind her ear. "I'm sorry. I never meant to lie to you. I didn't know, either," she said. James nodded, only beginning to understand how confusing this must have been for her. "So am I allowed in the car, or do you only date gennies?" Cody asked sweetly.

"I don't care what the List says—you'll always be my one," James said, pulling Cody closer for another kiss. When they finally came up for air, she had a huge smile on her face. "Unless you already joined the Equality Movement," James joked.

"No, I figure you could probably use a bodyguard right now."

"It's going to be pretty sweet for you, huh? You can get rid of your ID card, probably race in the meet on Friday, too."

Cody pulled away. "Yeah, I hadn't thought of that. I guess I still think of myself as a One in spirit. But I should probably stop."

As she climbed into his car and he started the engine, James realized how hard this was going to be for Cody. So much of her identity was tied up in her pride at being a One and in defending their rights. She had recently seemed like she was on the edge of doing something crazy, so James was grateful that this would pull her out of the chaos and maybe prevent a fight or confrontation that could ruin her life.

"I guess this means you won't be bombing any buildings with the Weather Channel then?" he said.

Cody looked at him—a little offended, it seemed. "Well, about that . . ."

"Cody, you can't—"

"It's a serious problem, James. They're pissed. They think I am some kind of spy."

"Oh, come on, if you just explain what happened—you went to *one* meeting, which they made you attend! They need to leave you alone."

But James knew this was going to be a tricky situation. He had spent only a few minutes around those people, but it was long enough to see they were serious, paranoid, and in possession of guns. Not exactly the ideal group to catch you in a lie.

"Maybe I don't want them to leave me alone."

"What?"

"I still believe everything I believed about the Ones two days ago. I still think what's happening is outrageous. Even more so after this list. And I still want to contribute to this fight. The Weathermen are taking action, and I want to be part of that."

"But Cody . . . you're not a One anymore," James said. He immediately knew his statement had come out wrong, in a mean way, instead of just a simple declaration of fact.

"No, I'm not, I get it. But what kind of person would I be if I changed all my morals because of that?" Cody paused for a second. "They asked me to prove my allegiance, James, and I am going to do it. Now I just need to figure out how."

James sighed, accepting the futility of fighting with her. Cody was still Cody. In one sense, it was a huge relief. He loved that fiery girl who wanted to change the world for the better. But the world was different now, and trying to change it was probably going to be very dangerous. James didn't even want to imagine what she might cook up to prove herself.

He also couldn't stop thinking about the package he saw at his father's office, the one shipped by the National Institutes of Health. In his gut, he knew this was something he should share with Cody. The NIH was something that the Ones talked about all the time, because it was the federal body that administered their pilot program. Every year they had to send in reams of data about their height and weight and blood pressure and triglyceride levels and everything else you could measure in the body. It wasn't much of a nuisance—everyone's doctor basically did it for them—but the NIH was still something that was always part of their life. James knew Cody had the tests done, too, but now he assumed her mother never mailed the results anywhere. Still, on a normal day, if James had gotten a weird feeling after seeing a package from the NIH, he would definitely loop Cody in on it.

But today was different. It was their first day together when Cody wasn't a One. It was a day when Cody was looking for a way to prove herself to the New Weathermen. And it was a day when telling her about a suspicious package in his father's lab didn't seem like a good thing to add into the mix.

=

The atmosphere at school was a little calmer than the day before. Marco and his cohorts were not prowling the parking lot with bounty posters. Sympathetic friends weren't rushing up with breathless warnings. When James and Cody walked in together, there were a few looks, sure, but it seemed that people were starting to move on from List Day. Anyway, James knew that in the grand scheme of the whole world, his high school was pretty safe. Obviously, the vast majority of the students weren't Ones, but most of them were still supportive of their peers in the minority. There were bad apples and bullies, but the younger generation was generally fine with the Ones. Knowing them, growing up with them, dating them, and being friends with them—James supposed it all made it harder to support their persecution. And his classmates weren't so freaked out by the technology, either. To them, genetic engineering was just another fancy gadget that had existed all their lives. It was the older generations that felt the most threatened. James knew this dynamic had existed in every generation since the apes looked disapprovingly at the cavemen, but this was different. Normal, upstanding adults—hell, even members of the Supreme Court—wanted to get rid of him. These people were the supposed silent majority in favor of the Equality Act. So, notwithstanding the recent experiences of being forced off a cliff and then almost pummeled in the parking lot, James felt he was safest around people his own age.

Today James and Cody had calculus together during first period, and they settled into their seats, relieved to be back in normal life. That normality lasted all of thirty seconds, however, because a blaring announcement came over the school PA system. Just like the week before, Margie's voice started calling out names to come immediately to the office. And just like last week, the names were all Ones. James stood up and gathered his things, frustrated. But unlike last time, Cody didn't join him.

"Punch Ms. Bixley in the nose for me, will you?" Cody said, only half-joking.

"I'll tell her you say hello."

"Actually, do me a favor," Cody said, reaching into her bag. "Give her this." She handed James her ID card.

James took the ID from Cody and couldn't help but sheepishly look down at his own, hanging around his neck.

"You should give her yours, too," Cody said.

"Let's see what she wants. I'll fill you in after class," James said, and then departed for the office.

When he got there, James joined the usual roundup. Laura, impeccably dressed. Gregory, his muscles a little more concealed than normal, perhaps in deference to the List coming out. Victor, fiddling with his Rubik's Cube. And the half-dozen others with whom James shared a nod of commiseration. Like last time, they waited forever before Ms. Bixley emerged from her office. Margie, ever the sweetheart, passed around her candy.

Ms. Bixley finally came out, carrying a folder. She stood in front of the Ones, smiling wider than usual.

"An interesting week, to say the least," she started. "As you know, we here at the school are committed to making sure all of our students are safe. And frankly, that's become a little more challenging. We are getting a lot of calls, a lot of complaints since the List came out. Threats, really. Some of them are anonymous; some of them are from parents. I'll be honest with you: Many people don't like the idea of you still being allowed in school."

James couldn't believe this. Fine, he could believe there were people looking for any and all ways to lash out at Ones, but he couldn't believe that prohibiting them from attending school was actually something being considered.

"Surely you understand we don't want to create an atmosphere of violence here on campus," Ms. Bixley continued. "And although I can see their point, I don't think barring you from school is the answer, either. So I've devised a way to ease tensions a little bit."

Ms. Bixley opened her folder and started handing sheets of paper to each student.

"The goal is to show everyone that those of you on the List are not getting any special advantage, and to help you demonstrate some humility, some appreciation for being tolerated here. If you all look down at your new schedules, you'll see we've replaced your lunch period with a community-service class. I'm sure that participating in this new class will send a powerful message to the whole town: No student has special privileges here. It's an opportunity to extend an olive branch to the rest of the school. And in doing so, we can hopefully avoid some of the ugly incidents that are happening elsewhere."

James and the rest of the Ones looked at Ms. Bixley in shock.

"So please report to Mr. Roland in the maintenance office at noon. And make sure to wear your ID cards so we know everyone is attending. Thanks, folks." And with that, Ms. Bixley smiled one last time and walked back into her office.

=

Mr. Roland was more commonly known as Tommy the Janitor. His patchy beard and angry mumbling identified him as the number one potential ax murderer in the West. How he still had a job at the school was beyond James's comprehension. Janitorial tenure was an odd and scary thing.

The "maintenance office" was actually a shed behind the gymnasium. When James and the rest of the Ones showed up at noon, Tommy was waiting for them, spitting tobacco juice into a soda bottle. They entered the cramped, dusty building, and Tommy began to clap his hands mockingly.

"Look at these special volunteers," he said with a sneer. "Boy, am I glad you kids offered to help."

Tommy paced in front of them, eyeing each One with naked disdain, and then he stopped in front of Laura. James saw her hands start to shake ever so slightly. Laura was an easy target, and James disliked the superior air with which she carried herself, but he did have a little sympathy at the moment. Students made U-turns in hallways to avoid Tommy, so having him stare at you from six inches away was a legit reason to freak out.

"Perfect. What a *perfect* way to start our community service," Tommy said to Laura. "Is that gum you are chewing?"

Laura immediately stopped chewing her gum. "Oh. It was."

"I thought it was against the rules to chew gum in school," Tommy said.

"I didn't mean to."

"You didn't mean to put gum in your mouth?"

"I didn't mean to break a rule. I'm sorry."

"Give it to me." Tommy stuck his hand right under Laura's mouth.

Laura shook her head uncomfortably. She looked around at the rest of the Ones. James wished he could do something, but he was also kind of enjoying this.

"Give it to me!" Tommy shouted.

"It's gone."

Tommy gave her a twisted smile, backed off, and started pacing again. "If only the rest of you animals were as considerate as . . ."

"Laura."

"As Laura. But no, you're not. Where does everyone else get rid of their gum?" Tommy paused for a second. "ON THE FUCKING GROUND!" he roared.

James and the others staggered back from the outburst. Tommy was jumping around erratically now, working himself into a froth.

"Today we are going to fix that problem. We are going to find all the gum, scrape all the gum, and get rid of all the gum! Does that sound like a good plan?"

A few of the Ones nodded, trying to be agreeable. Tommy went to a drawer and then came back and handed rusty scraping tools to each student.

"Your first assignment in community-service class is to start in the lunch yard. Good Lord, do you kids love some gum after lunch. Now go. Find each piece and make it disappear." Tommy grabbed his bottle of tobacco juice and stormed out of the maintenance shed in a huff.

=

Wednesday it was the gum. They crawled around on their hands and knees scraping the hard black spots off the walkways. The rest of the school watched in uncomfortable awe.

Marco, of course, couldn't resist walking over and spitting a wad of gum right next to James. "Amber Reed says thanks," he said, sneering. James didn't give him the satisfaction of a reaction.

Cody, on the other hand, upon seeing James and some of her other friends forced into this absurd act, joined them in solidarity. She got right down next to the Ones and started scraping away.

This obviously drove Ms. Bixley crazy, because she rushed over and stood above Cody with a scowl. "What are you doing?"

Cody barely looked up. "Community service."

A few other students who were also sympathetic to the Ones walked over and began cleaning the floor, too. Cody and James shared a smile, delighted at this growing act of disobedience.

"Stop it!" Ms. Bixley yelled, scurrying among the kneeling students. "You are not part of this class!"

James and Cody and everyone else kept working. It was the most enjoyable manual labor they had ever done.

On Thursday it was beautification of the school entrance. A row of dead bushes had to be dug up and replaced with new ones. But the Ones' schedule had changed again. They no longer had community service during lunch, when all the other students were free. Now they had been pulled out of a regular class period, and there was no one around to join them. Ms. Bixley watched them with glee as they exerted themselves on the messy lawn.

On Friday it was the floor of the kitchen. The work was made even more miserable because Congress had officially passed the Equality Act that morning. The Ones heard the news as they mopped and bleached and polished a decade's worth of spills and mold. James simultaneously cursed the government and swore off eating school food ever again.

By this point, some of the Ones had told their parents what was going on. The adults found it hard to believe, of course, but today Laura's father came by to see for himself. When he saw the Ones cleaning the kitchen floor, he stormed off to Bixley's office. A few minutes later he came back in a rage.

"Let's go," he said, walking over to Laura and plowing his shoulder through Tommy the Janitor. "You're done with this piece-of-shit school."

The other students watched uncomfortably as Laura rushed out with her father. James never saw her in school again, which summed up their options pretty neatly: Put up with this hour-long indignity or hide yourself away.

After school, with their hellish week coming to an end, the Ones gathered and decided they couldn't take it anymore. If Ms. Bixley had set out to humiliate them, she had succeeded. But she had also united them. United them in anger toward her and in their determination to fight back. Even James, who for months had been preaching the logic of keeping their heads down, had come around.

Although their frustration level was universal, they couldn't agree on what to do next. The obvious answer was to simply refuse to participate in this community-service charade, but Ms. Bixley had assured them that this was very much a class and that their academic records would be ruined if they tried such a stunt. And even though other students had tried to join them at first, Cody was the only one who kept trying, sneaking out of class when she could. By the third day, the novelty had worn off and most of the students barely noticed them anymore. Peering out a window and seeing the Ones doing grunt work around the school? Yeah, that just made sense now. The fact that people were starting to consider this the new normal was chilling.

The Ones couldn't settle on a plan, though, and James grew frustrated.

Against his better judgment, he brought it up to Cody when he caught up with her a little later. Cody thought out loud, summarizing what she assumed they wanted to accomplish.

"You want to shove it in Ms. Bixley's face. You want to get rid of the community-service requirement. And you want to make a point that Ones need to be treated equally."

James nodded.

"Here's the thing," Cody continued. "The rest of the students, aside from the Bench Mob, agree with all of that. It's just Bixley and her army of bitter teachers who are making this happen."

"So what do we do? It's not like we run the school. We can't just snap our fingers and change these crazy new policies."

Cody, deep in thought, suddenly opened her eyes wide, and James could practically see the lightbulb above her head. She turned to him with a mischievous smile that was already making him nervous. But what choice did he have other than to turn to Cody? His school was trying to dehumanize him, and his family had admitted that his existence was a mistake. It was an ironic label for the son who was never allowed to mess up. If that was how everyone felt about him, then James was ready to stop living up to that impossible standard.

He prodded Cody to go on. "Whatever you're thinking, just say it."

"Maybe it's time we kill two birds with one stone," she said, her excitement obvious. "You want to protest Bixley's new rules for the Ones. I need to prove myself to Kai and the Weathermen."

James knew there was no stopping whatever came out of her mouth next, and he steeled himself to hop on board.

Cody's eyes were gleaming. "Let's take over the school."

CHAPTER 9

CODY AND JAMES spent all of Saturday hashing out a plan. With enough confederates, they could easily take over the administration building, blockade the doors, and then communicate their demands. Cody loved that their act of defiance would echo the student protests of the 1960s, the era that gave birth to the original Weather Underground. She and James agreed that no one was to get hurt. James was adamant on this point, and Cody recognized that they would need to keep the moral high ground to achieve any measure of success.

"Are you sure I can't just toss Ms. Bixley off the roof?" she asked wistfully.

"Cody," James growled a light warning. "No weapons and no tossing principals or teachers around. Promise?"

"Fine, fine."

They packed a duffel bag with everything a person might need to take over a high school, or at least what they thought they might need. Energy bars, some emergency gallons of water, and a few treats—marshmallows, brownie brittle, and pistachio nuts. Headlamps to navigate in the darkness. Ski goggles and bandannas. A change of clothes. A toolbox and first-aid kit. A laptop with a cellular Internet antenna. A bullhorn. A toothbrush.

And that crucial accessory everyone couldn't live without: cell-phone chargers.

They spent Sunday rallying the troops. James reached out to his fellow Ones and close friends. Cody got in touch with her crew from the cross-country team, some other science geeks, and anyone else she knew to be sympathetic to the Ones' cause. They all agreed to help, especially after Cody made the whole thing sound like equal parts party and protest.

When she left James's house that evening, she couldn't believe they were actually doing this. Her dream of fighting for justice with the boy she loved was finally coming true. Not exactly under the circumstances she had imagined, but Cody was still thrilled that James had come around. It seemed that the fancy-pants debate captain just needed to get his hands dirty to get a change of perspective.

As James walked Cody out of his house, he stopped suddenly and tugged on her hand. She turned around in surprise.

"You were right," he said.

"About what?"

"We can't sit around and do nothing."

Cody nodded, appreciating the gesture.

"I'm sorry I snapped at you outside the church last week. I still don't agree with all that revolution stuff, but you've been right all along: If we don't stand up for ourselves, who will?"

Cody smiled and took his hands in hers. "I will."

James smiled back. "You know what I mean. And besides, you're still as perfect and dislikable as the rest of us," he said, gesturing to her. "Seriously, look at you—who turns out like this without any help? Those lips, those legs, that face . . . it's ridiculous!"

Cody tried to smack him, but James caught her and pulled her close. They kissed good-night, parted, and wouldn't see each other again until noon the next day in the school office. They were ready to make some trouble.

=

Two minutes after noon, they crashed through the doors of the main office, and the first thing they did was go for the telephones. Cody hopped over Margie's elevated desk and yanked the large phone unit out of the wall.

"Excuse me . . ." Margie said as she reflexively rolled her chair into the safety of a corner.

Cody was already past her, past the faculty mailboxes, where Mr. Oberlee and Mr. Alvarez were sorting their mail. Past the guidance counselor's office, which she glanced into and saw James ripping out a phone. Cody smashed through an office door and came face-to-face with Ms. Bixley.

Ms. Bixley was standing at her desk, poking furiously at her phone as she held the receiver to her ear. Cody raced across the room.

"This is Leila Bixley from Shasta High School. We are—"

Cody smashed her fist down on the phone, ending the call. She took the whole unit, pulled the receiver away from Ms. Bixley, walked over to the window, and tossed everything outside.

"What the hell do you think you're doing?"

"Taking over your school. Now, get out of my way."

Cody went to a shelf behind Ms. Bixley's desk. She opened her purse, found her cell phone, and tossed it out the window, as well.

"You stupid little brat. You are making the biggest mistake of your life."

Cody calmly walked over to her. She duplicated the same sinister smile Ms. Bixley had flashed to her last week.

"It's all right to be scared about what's happening. You should be."

Cody broke into a smile of joy and made her way back out to the administration area. Students had already shut the nearest staircase doors that led outside, and they were moving desks in front of them. The phones had all been disconnected. James walked around collecting any spare cell phones from the adults. Margie looked like she was in shock. Ms. Bixley remained in her office. Mr. Oberlee and Mr. Alvarez were still pinned against their mailboxes. Gregory stood in front of them, preventing anyone from leaving.

Cody and several other students went back into the hallway and made their way quickly to the library. She pulled the fire alarm on the way, and by the time they entered, a handful of students and librarians were rushing down the stairs to leave. When it was totally clear, they barricaded the doors to the main staircase so there was no other way in or out. They had fully locked down their own little section of campus: the two-story administration building, the covered walkway to the library, and the main floor of the library. Their home base was now secure.

Back in the office area, James had confined the four adults in the cramped quarters of the guidance counselor's office. Cody got back there just in time to see him shut the door. She put a hand on his shoulder and nodded.

"Phase one of the plan . . . all good so far," Cody said.

Then she went over to Margie's desk and grabbed the public-address microphone. Cody clicked it on and heard the buzzing come through over the speakers. She was about to address the entire school.

"Attention, everyone. This is Cody Bell. I am proud to inform you that a group of students has taken over the school."

James and some of the others moved over to the windows, where they watched everyone outside come to a standstill as they listened to the announcement.

Cody continued. "We have done this to ensure the rights and safety of our fellow students, especially those who have been singled out for persecution. We believe in the true definition of equality, and we will not leave until the current school leaders are replaced by an administration that also agrees to ensure it. We have not hurt anyone, and we will not hurt anyone. This is a peaceful protest. We ask that all who support us in this cause come to the library immediately. Everyone else can go home. School is dismissed."

Cody clicked off the microphone and relished in this power for a moment. It reminded her of hearing Kai's speech back at the church. She wasn't just sitting on her hands—she was taking action and inspiring others to do the same. When she joined everyone else at the window, she saw students pouring out of classes, gathering in front of the administration building, and looking up at the second floor. Her heart soared.

"What do we do now?" James asked.

Victor spoke up. "They want to see us. To believe this is real."

James turned to Cody. "Go ahead, give them a wave or something."

Cody stepped up to the window and opened it. But instead of sticking her head outside, she turned back to James. "No. It has to be one of you."

Cody moved aside for James to get near the window. He hesitated for a moment and then leaned his torso outside and raised a single finger to the sky. The students below him went nuts.

The rest of the afternoon passed in a blur of finalizing the security of their setup. First, they had to let a mass of new kids into the library. Cody couldn't be sure if these students shared the same ideals or just wanted to hang out, but the atmosphere in the two occupied buildings was of unified excitement. They all got to work rebarricading the entrance points, and then it slowly began to dawn on them that there was nothing else to do. And of course, in a giant room full of books, not one was removed from a shelf. Cody saw this boredom and uncertainty start to set in and realized that they may have to accelerate their timeline.

They had planned somewhat for this, and she had asked Victor to set up some wireless speakers and then put her friend Erica in charge of the playlist. Within minutes, some old-school Beastie Boys began to blast, and Erica was trying to start a dance party. She had already dragged James's friend Andrew out of his seat, and Cody tried not to laugh at his awkward dance moves. She was relieved that people were embracing the takeover, but she knew the party atmosphere was only a temporary distraction. She and James had made plans to continue the occupation for the long haul, for as many days as it took. The support of their fellow students would last only so long, though.

The cops had already arrived and arranged a line of cars in front of the administration building. Granted, it was only four cars from the local department, but Cody knew more would be coming. She had hoped they'd send everything they had, all those tanks and trucks that seemed to have no purpose but had been left over from one war or another. Seeing those monstrosities attack kids on a high school campus was bound to wake up at least some members of the silent, accommodating majority. Cody's cell phone had already buzzed several times with a number that she assumed was a police line. But before she talked to them, she wanted to have a different conversation.

Cody walked up to the small office where all the adults were being held. Gregory was standing in the doorway, arms crossed like a bouncer. She tried not to laugh, but Cody appreciated that Gregory was trying to do his part. Even she was a little intimidated by his size.

"Can you bring Ms. Bixley to her office so I can talk to her?" she asked the self-appointed head of security. Gregory nodded, and Cody went to wait.

When Gregory ushered Ms. Bixley into her own office, Cody was seated comfortably behind the desk. She pointed at a chair.

"Have a seat."

Ms. Bixley sat down, staring at Cody, eyes burning. Cody nodded for Gregory to leave.

"You listened to our announcement, right?"

Ms. Bixley nodded. "If your plan is to accomplish nothing, get expelled, and go to jail, you kids really nailed it."

"Call the school superintendent, offer your resignation, and everyone goes home safely. School picks right up again tomorrow morning. Without you."

"You know I'm not going to do that."

"Then get comfortable. Because we are not leaving until you do."

Ms. Bixley eyed Cody with utter disdain. "You're even more pathetic than I thought. All you care about is the attention. About finding some way to make people think you're special. Well, that list proved that you're nothing but a liar. You want to be a martyr so badly, though, that even when it was taken away from you, you'll do anything to get it back. That's not being a martyr, Cody. That's being a slut for attention."

For an instant, Cody couldn't help herself. She leaped across the room and was about to knock Ms. Bixley right out of her chair. But just in the nick of time, she remembered that this wasn't about punishing Ms. Bixley. This was about making a clear and intelligent statement about justice for her peers. She could ruin the whole thing by leaving the slightest mark on Ms. Bixley's infuriating face. So she stopped herself.

Cody walked out of the office and found Gregory. "Put her back in with the others."

She continued on and found the rest of the Ones milling about in the office atrium, mostly just eating the candy from Margie's bowl.

Cody peeked out the window and saw that the armada of police vehicles had grown. It wasn't just local cop cars now; there were also SWAT trucks, FBI vans, and most conspicuously, a large black "school" bus with bars over the windows. Things were getting interesting.

Cody turned to Victor, their tech ace. "Did you e-mail out the statement?"

Victor nodded. "Yup. To the local precinct and all the news stations. And it's posted on our Facebook group."

"We have a Facebook group?" James asked.

"Of course. The Likes are rolling in." Victor paused. "A few angry comments from some parents, but I am deleting those."

"What about the Board of Education . . . any response?" Cody asked.

"No. Just the cops demanding that we leave the premises peacefully."

"Reiterate that we're not budging unless the people who

run this school and support discrimination against their own students are replaced. Until then, it looks like it's gonna be a long night. Let's go double-check the exits and start passing out some food," Cody said.

The Ones headed off in different directions. Cody grabbed a bag full of cereal bars and headed down the walkway to the library. The kids there had turned it into a giant lounge. Music still played, study tables had been pushed aside, and everyone was just hanging out and looking through the giant windows at the gathering circus outside. As Cody weaved her way through the students, a few of them offered a fist bump or a "good job." At the very least, everyone seemed pleased that there was no school tomorrow. Cody was in the middle of tossing out cereal bars when her phone buzzed with a text.

"PQ3318" flashed on her screen.

Cody smiled, a quick jolt of excitement running through her body as if by reflex. She looked up toward the second floor of the library, dropped her bag, and practically ran up the stairs.

When Cody had gone deep enough into the stacks and found the right aisle, James was already waiting in their spot.

"A little bit easier this time," he said.

She walked up to him and kissed him, hard.

James stroked a lock of hair away from her face. "We did it. We really did it," he said.

"I know. I'm so happy for you."

"For us. You made it happen."

"But for you especially. All this bullshit you've been dealing with at school, being treated like a criminal—it's over. We're gonna stop it for good. And I know we're gonna get in trouble in other ways, but it will be worth it. They can't keep doing what they've been doing."

James nodded. "It feels good. Getting in trouble, I mean. I guess you always knew that."

Cody's phone started to buzz, but she ignored it and looked back at James. "It suits you," she said, and kissed him again, sticking her hands under his shirt and tracing the contours of his torso. "This whole hot-altar-boy thing you've been pulling off needed a tweak."

"Oh yeah? Well, I assume we are all officially America's Most Wanted by now. I'm glad you like that." James's phone started going off, too, but he silenced it.

Cody ran her fingers through his hair. "Well, the *wanted* part is right."

As the two pressed into each other, both their phones wouldn't stop buzzing. Cody finally gave in and looked at it.

"Oh my God."

"What?" James asked, and reached for his phone, too.

They clicked on the same photo that clearly had been seen by the entire world by now. It was taken in the office area they had just left. Margie, the school secretary, was standing on a chair that was balanced precariously on top of a second chair. She had a look of pure terror on her face. Her hands were bound.

And around her neck was a noose tied to the ceiling.

"What the hell is this?" James shouted. "Did you do this?"

"No! I would never! We agreed no one would get hurt, remember?"

"Jesus, it's already going viral. The cops'll think we're about to kill her!"

"I didn't do it, James, I swear!"

"Then who the hell did?" he yelled.

A voice spoke up from behind them. "I did."

Cody and James jerked their heads around as they heard someone else step into their aisle.

It was Kai.

CHAPTER 10

"WHAT THE HELL are they doing here?" James hissed at Cody as Kai walked up to them. Following right behind him was Taryn, the girl whom James had last encountered pressing a gun into his head.

"I know you're upset about the photo—let me explain," Kai said.

James grabbed Cody. "Seriously, why are they here?"

He could see from Cody's face that she was surprised, too. "I told Kai about the takeover," she said. "But I didn't know that they would—"

"We're here to keep an eye on things," Taryn said. "And on people," she added, glaring at Cody.

James could barely keep up with who was angry at whom. But he was definitely pissed at Cody for looping these maniacs into their plan. If the headlines from around the country were true and the New Weathermen were responsible for everything attributed to them, the group seemed to know only one speed—full throttle. But what James and the rest of the students were doing at the school needed a delicate touch. They were trying to prove a point—not trying to get arrested. Now that the Equality Act had passed, James knew what could happen to Ones who were arrested. Anything, essentially. They were subject to thirty days of detention without being charged or getting access to a lawyer. Sure, that trampled on the basic principles of the country's legal system, but apparently people would accept anything dressed up in the name of public safety. So now that the leaders of the militant underground Ones were in on the job, James suddenly saw his freedom at stake.

"You guys need to leave," James said. "This is a student protest. We don't need your group getting involved."

"By all means," Kai said. "We want to let you guys lead. Cody looped us in on the plan, and we came by the school and walked into the library with everyone else. We just want to help in any way we can."

Cody shoved her phone in Kai's face. The picture of Margie strung up by the noose was still on the screen. "This is what you call helping? We had things going perfectly, and now you have us killing the school secretary. Everyone loves her!"

"No one is getting killed. We set up the photo, and then

we took her down, gave her a pat on the ass, and put her back in the office. She's fine," Taryn said.

"And as much as we appreciate the job you are doing, everything is not going perfectly," Kai added.

"What do you mean?" James said.

"Well, what's next?" Kai said.

"They have our demands. Either they meet them or we wait," said Cody.

"Until they cut the power and the water? Within a few hours, you'll have a mutiny on your hands, and a few hours after that, even you will be begging to leave."

"All right, if we need your help so badly, what's your brilliant suggestion?" James asked.

"We need to provoke a response," Kai said.

James turned to Cody and shook his head. "*We?* Do you hear him? Is this what you wanted all along?"

"No. I wanted to do this alone. To prove myself, remember? But they're here now, and they're on our side—let's just listen," she said.

James couldn't believe this. He had never seen Cody submit like this. Certainly not to him. But here she was, gladly agreeing to abdicate her leadership to someone she barely knew.

"Look, guys, here's the truth," Kai said. "These protests can go two ways. They can go as planned and make a nice little point. Or they can get ugly and make a real statement. The assholes waiting outside are dying to come in here and bust some heads. That's just who they are—it's no fun to get all the body armor and shields and night vision if you don't get to use it. And it will look pretty good for us if they come in smashing doors and windows and trampling all these students. But we have to give them a reason."

"And get someone hurt? I'm not signing off on that," James said.

"No sacrificial lambs, I agree. We'll tell everyone to protect themselves and film as much as they can on their phones. The optics will still look really bad for the guys outside," Kai said.

As much as James didn't want to admit it, he saw Kai's point. There was the potential for their little protest to affect more than just one school. The images of cops running roughshod through a high school would be pretty powerful—maybe enough to sway some people back to the side of the Ones.

"But what about the fact that they think we're hanging the school secretary? Isn't that enough to get us arrested?" he asked.

Kai shook his head. "They'll see she's fine. No harm, no foul. Besides, you can always blame it on the Weathermen if you get caught."

Cody raised her eyebrows in surprise. "What? You want us to blame you?"

Taryn snorted. "Stuff gets blamed on us every day. Just don't use our names."

James considered this. It actually did give them an out if anything truly bad happened.

He looked at Cody and nodded, conceding the point.

"All right. So by now they've seen the photo you posted. What's next?" James asked.

"They are going to come hard, and they are going to come soon. We need to make it as difficult as possible for them and reinforce the barricade in the office," Kai said, and then turned to Cody. "You and I should get back there and get started—we don't have much time."

James was annoyed—why was that an exclusively Kai-and-Cody mission? "Shouldn't we all go?" he asked.

"No, you stay here with Taryn. She can tell the rest of the students how to handle the incursion so they don't get hurt. You and Cody know the school . . . we need you to split up."

Cody touched James on the arm. "It's fine. Let's just get ready as quickly as possible," she said. Kai had already started walking away, and she rushed off after him.

James was left alone with Taryn. She looked around disapprovingly at the bookshelves.

"What the hell were you doing back here?" she asked.

"What do you think?" James said, irritated.

"I think you need to reevaluate this little puppy-love thing you've got going on."

"What does that mean?"

"That girl is a liar. If you're a One and you care about our fight, you can't trust her."

"Believe me, Cody is just as committed as any of you. This isn't some long con for her."

"We'll see, won't we? It's nothing I can't handle if you're wrong," Taryn said. Then she shook her head in exasperation. "Kai is really cautious, and he knows what he's doing—except when he's thinking with his dick."

James glared at Taryn. "That's why he's here?"

"Like he said, this is a great protest opportunity. But Kai is a stickler for efficiency. Mixing business with pleasure is right up his alley," Taryn said, and started walking away. "Come on, let's go teach these kids how to crawl under some tear gas."

James stood alone in the row of books, and his eye caught the spine label of PQ3318. This secret spot in the library suddenly wasn't so romantic anymore. He was starting to feel ready to punch something—if not Kai, then a wall might do. He hurried to catch up with Taryn.

"So was Kai in the military or something before?" James asked as he and Taryn walked through the library.

"No. He was in reform school for a bit. I guess that's kind of similar."

"Reform school? Like for criminals and idiots who flunked out of high school?"

"Yeah. This place was no joke. I'm talking fight-for-your-blanket type of situation."

"Born a One and you end up there? That's pretty embarrassing."

"Why's that?" Taryn asked quickly. "Ones can't ever make a mistake?"

"They shouldn't," James said, knowing from his own experience that this standard was possible to achieve, even if it wasn't the most pleasant way to grow up. "You win the genetic lottery, have every advantage in the world, and you still can't make something of yourself? I find that pathetic."

Taryn looked at him with disgust. "Well, maybe if you understood what he went through in there, you'd be a little more sympathetic."

James waved her off dismissively. "What did he do to get sent there?"

"It was more like something his mom did. She entered the NIH lottery, won a spot, and had her baby genetically engineered without telling Kai's dad. She eventually fessed up when Kai was ten, and the dad went apeshit. Started clobbering Kai and never stopped."

"So Kai ran away or something?"

"No. Kai grew up and *made* him stop."

James thought about how intense that must have been, then considered how being a One had affected his own family. It was uncomfortable, but apparently it was nothing like the rift that existed for other families. And sure, his brother had grown so combative that James finally had to hurt him, but his fight with Michael had seemed like a natural extension of their normal sibling rivalry. He could never imagine doing that to his father.

If Taryn was telling the truth, Kai did more than imagine it.

"I guess that explains his sunny disposition," James said. "And what about you? When did you two first team up?"

"I'd tell you . . . but I think you'd find it 'pathetic.'"

Taryn walked ahead of him and descended to the main floor of the library. James watched her go, and despite the very real animosity he harbored for this girl, he suddenly felt like a total jerk.

=

After James and Taryn had warned and prepared the students staying in the library, they made their way back to the main office. The barricades had been bolstered and were pretty ingeniously designed now. The furniture blocking the entrance was now buttressed by desks that went all the way back to the opposite wall. Simply barging through was not going to be possible. James and Taryn slipped through a crack that had been left for them. The four of them, the rest of the Ones, and the four adults were hunkered down.

James saw Cody and Kai over by the window and went to join them. They were staring down at the marshaling forces outside. It was clear the cops were moving around with more urgency.

"What are they doing?" James asked.

"Treating it like a hostage situation," Kai said. "They think we might kill that lady, and since we're not answering any of their calls, they have no choice but to storm the building."

James nodded toward the office holding the adults. "They're fine?"

"I checked, all good," Cody said. "Margie seemed flattered to have a starring role. Mr. Oberlee offered to mediate for us. I feel bad that he was stuck here when we came in—he has little kids at home."

"And Ms. Bixley?"

"Still a bitch."

James watched as Kai patted Cody on the back. "All right, we should probably get going. You'll be fine, Cody. Just stay cool and call me later," Kai said.

"What the hell are you talking about?" James asked.

Kai laughed. "You think we're just going to wait here until the cops bust in and then surrender? Come on, they can detain Ones forever now without charges. They'll lock us up in a basement somewhere. You too. Let's go, we've got to get out of here and mix in with everyone else in the library."

"It's just a student protest. The cops might put us in jail for the night, but we won't be charged under the Equality Act," James argued.

"Of course we will. Especially if they think we are the leaders," Taryn said.

"So who's going to take the fall, then?" James asked.

No one spoke for a moment. James realized they all knew the answer already. He finally caught on and looked at Cody.

"No." He grabbed her arm. "You can't do this. It's not fair."

"James—"

"I'm staying with you. I won't let you go down for this."

"James, just listen. If you all get caught here, you're screwed. If it's only me, sure I'll be in trouble, but they can't charge me as a One. I'll just show them the List, right? And besides, we haven't done anything serious. We just moved some furniture around in our school. I'll be fine."

James could barely believe what he was hearing. Kai must have talked her into this while James and Taryn were still in the library. Or Cody could have been leaning this way all along to prove herself to the Weathermen. And as for Kai and Taryn . . . of course they were too smart to not have an escape hatch.

Even worse for his pride, the idea actually made sense. Cody was the only person involved who might be treated fairly by the legal system. James knew there was no point in keeping her company just to look brave.

Taryn tapped the window. "They're moving in. We gotta go."

James stepped up to Cody and grabbed her by the shoulders. "I'm going to kill you for this. Promise me you'll be smart and stay safe?"

"I promise. You too."

James leaned in to give Cody a passionate kiss, not caring that Kai and Taryn were there. Or maybe he was happy that they were watching. When he finally pulled back, Cody give him a wink, and they let go of each other.

James saw that Kai looked a little pissed as he walked over to the barricaded door and started ushering the rest of the Ones out through the tiny crawl space. Cody would be able to fill it back in after they left and seal the entrance again. When it was just James and Kai left, James gestured grandly for Kai to go first. If he wasn't going to stay with Cody, he would at least be the last person to leave her.

They made their way back to the library and joined the rest of the students. Everyone was pressed against the floor-to-ceiling windows, watching as a SWAT team approached the school, their phones held high to film it. James found the scene totally riveting as the cops charged ahead in formation, shields in front of them, assault rifles ready, their shiny black helmets making them look like a brigade of militarized bugs. He had to remind himself that what he was watching wasn't just pure spectacle for his entertainment—these people were coming for him.

James was craning his neck and watching the SWAT team approach the front of the library when the first flash grenade went off. The explosion left him totally deaf, save for a ringing in his ears. And even though his eyes didn't work temporarily, he knew it made no sense: The SWAT team was still outside, but the students in the library were already under attack.

When his sight and hearing began to return, James could sense that another SWAT team had come in through a back entrance and was now stampeding right through them. He could sense people screaming at him over and over again.

"Everybody down!"

"Hands on your head!"

"Don't move!"

Across the room, James saw Andrew, obviously dazed, try to lift himself to stand. James tried to shout at him to stay down, but he was too late. A SWAT guy swung a rifle butt into the back of Andrew's head and left him lying motionless. James tried to melt himself into the floor, hating himself for letting his friend get hurt.

Then the other SWAT team from out front emerged at the top of the staircase, and James saw them rush through the newly secured library and into the hallway connected to the administration building. He knew what awaited them there: a single doorway made almost impenetrable by Kai's clever barricade. But they would find a way through somehow, James knew that. And then they'd find Cody. James just hoped she was in a mood to listen.

In the meantime, the cops in the library were starting to round up all the students and guide them outside. James fell into line near Kai and Taryn, and they were rushed down the stairs and out to the lawn in front of the school. The cops kept herding them toward the parking lot, where all the cars were parked, sirens flashing. And just beyond that, James saw the black school bus with steel bars over its windows—the police were directing them right into it. It felt like a fire drill to prison.

Then, as they were crossing the lawn, there was a tremendous explosion from behind them. James turned around and saw the last flashes blow out the windows from the second floor of the administration building. Exactly where Cody was trapped.

James felt the urge to break the line of students and rush back to the building, but the line no longer existed. Everyone was screaming and running in different directions. Sparks and smoke started to filter down. The cops kept trying to direct them, but it was of no use. The students were running away in pure chaos.

James turned around to go back, but Taryn grabbed his shoulder.

"Don't," Taryn said. "Now is our chance." She gestured sideways to a narrow space between a classroom building and the gym. Kai was already sprinting toward it, fighting against the stream of all the other kids, his instincts attuned to act right away.

James took another look at the administration building. He could see from their headlamps that the SWAT team had infiltrated the offices. Cody was either blown to bits or in handcuffs. He wheeled around and started sprinting after Kai and Taryn.

They were fast, but James was faster. And he knew the school better, so when he caught up with them between buildings and they emerged at the rear boundary of the school, James took the lead and raced toward Tommy's maintenance shed. It was a low building on the edge of campus. If they got on the roof, they could hop over the school's back fence and slip into the woods. And James knew there would be a ladder lying around.

As they sprinted up to the shed, a flashlight illuminated them from behind.

"Don't move, or I'll shoot you!"

James ignored the command and lifted the ladder against the shed.

"Stop! Police!" A cop was running up to them, but all James could see was a bouncing beam of light.

"Go!" Kai said, and pushed James and Taryn up the ladder.

James pulled himself onto the roof and then helped Taryn up. He heard the sound of a brutal collision below.

151

James looked over the edge and saw Kai and the cop rolling around on the ground. The cop was big, but Kai had pinned him down and was raining blows down on his head. He dazed him with a punch and had enough time to leap up and get away. But instead of climbing up the ladder, Kai took a heavy gardening shovel from the wall of the shed. He walked back to the cop and bashed him over the head with it. James, standing above, staggered back just from seeing the impact. The cop collapsed in a heap, totally still. James froze in shock. Had Kai just killed a police officer?

Without skipping a beat, Kai tossed the shovel, shimmied up the ladder, knocked it off the roof, and was the first one of them to scale down the fence and make it off the school grounds. James stared after him in horror, and Taryn had to shout in his ear and shove him before he followed. His flight response took over. Within seconds, they had concealed themselves in the thick trees. They jogged steadily for a while, away from the school and the confluence of the authorities.

After about thirty minutes, they reached an old logging road that led from the outskirts of town up the mountain. James recognized it from some of the summers he'd spent volunteering with the local wildfire-prevention crew. He had never minded the backbreaking work; it just felt great to be outdoors and do something important. The crew cleared brush, did some controlled burns, and tried to keep their beautiful tinderbox of a home as safe as possible. Now he was walking around the same woods like a fugitive.

Once they slowed down, James angled over to Kai and asked him something that had been gnawing at him while they ran. "Is that cop back there *dead*?"

"He'll be fine. I saw him roll over before I jumped," Kai said.

"It seemed like he was—"

"Send him some flowers, okay? We've got a long hike. Let's just shut up."

Kai walked away briskly, clearly done with their chat. James turned to Taryn. "Where are we going?" he asked.

"This road leads up to the mine quarry. We can lie low there for the night," Taryn said.

"What about Cody?"

"There's nothing we can do for her right now. Come on."

"Why the quarry? We're just gonna go up there, stop, and lie down where everyone in town goes to party?"

Taryn laughed at him. "Seriously?" She saw that James wasn't joking. "Don't worry, there are plenty of places to hide in those mines. I thought every Shasta kid knew that."

James felt his cheeks burn with embarrassment. *Not every kid*, he thought, *not the ones whose siblings had drowned there and then had been born to replace them.* Granted, that was probably a pretty small group, but

James resented her presumption. Even so, he wasn't about to explain all of that to her.

James did, however, want to get something else off his chest. He was grateful that Taryn had forced him to sneak away during the stampede. And he knew he owed her an apology.

"Hey," he said as they marched on together. "I'm sure it wasn't easy being in that reform school. I shouldn't have been so judgmental about it. Sometimes I forget that not every kid grew up like I did. Even other Ones."

"Yeah, thanks," Taryn mumbled without looking at him.

"If you ever want to tell me more about it, I'd be curious to hear. You obviously got quite an education in there."

"What's that supposed to mean?" she asked, combatively.

James hadn't meant to insult her again, but damn was she prickly. "Look, you obviously know how to handle yourself in these situations. It's a little bit newer to me. All I'm saying is, if you have any pointers for me, I'm all ears."

"Oh. Okay," she said in a gentler tone. "I guess I might as well start with lesson number one: Don't keep your wallet in your back pocket, idiot."

James immediately felt for his wallet, but he already knew it was gone. Thankfully, Taryn was holding it out for him. He took it back sheepishly and slid it into his front pocket.

"Sometimes I just can't resist," she said. But then she smiled to show no hard feelings.

Taryn seemed like she was about to proceed to lesson two, but she didn't get the chance. Kai had come to a stop ahead of them. James and Taryn practically bumped into him as he stood perfectly still, staring at his phone. James could tell from his face that the news was horrible.

"What is it? Is she dead?" he yelled in a panic.

Kai looked up at him with eyes that burned with anger. "No. See for yourself."

James took the phone and read the news story that Kai had clicked on. It was an article about the SWAT incursion of the school takeover. James scanned the text quickly, but the headline made it clear enough.

Margie was dead and the cops were calling it a murder.

CHAPTER 11

HOURS HAD PASSED since she'd been arrested, but Cody still couldn't get the smell of gunpowder out of her nose. It wasn't just her nose; it was all five senses, really. She could taste it in her mouth. Her eyes burned. Her ears were still ringing. And she swore that her body was still vibrating from the first big explosion. She hadn't been injured in a conventional sense, but she had felt a wave of invisible force shake every cell in her body. That is what finally broke the office door down.

Cody had been so dazed from the SWAT team ordnance that she could barely remember what happened. She was pinned to the ground, a knee crushing her spine, and then handcuffed. Dragged out of the building. Thrown into a cop car and driven to the local police station. And now here she was, locked in an interrogation room by herself, having been ignored for what felt like several hours.

She rested her head on the cold metal table and tried to sleep. It was impossible, though; her mind was racing too fast. It wasn't fear that gripped her. She had mentally prepared herself for a night in jail, for having the cops condescend to her, even for the inevitable misdemeanor charge and her mother completely freaking out. What kept her from sleeping was a nervous anxiety that Cody couldn't really explain. She had the gnawing sense that something serious was happening on the other side of the locked steel door, that beyond the tiny bubble of her interrogation room, events were transpiring that had the power to change her life.

Cody hoped those events were positive. She engaged in some wishful thinking and imagined that their little stunt had gone viral across the country, that maybe they had inspired countless other schools to protest for the rights of Ones. Maybe one of the SWAT team members hit a student with his club, and it had been caught on camera. Maybe the Board of Education was firing Ms. Bixley at this very moment.

But Cody couldn't know any of that for sure, stuck as she was in this barren room, devoid of all stimuli. She was desperate for any indication and going mad with the realization that everyone else in the world besides her knew what was going on. For the first time, she considered the intensely punishing power of being confined in utter isolation.

Her prayers, such as they were, were finally answered when the door swung open and a tall, elegant woman in a fancy suit entered. Cody could tell she wasn't from Shasta and definitely had nothing to do with their local police force. She wore her short blond hair like any other government drone, but the expressiveness of her face indicated something else to Cody. This woman was clearly passionate about something, but in a scary, obsessive way. She had the look of a zealot.

"Cody, I am not here to bullshit you."

The woman entered, dropped a closed folder on the table, sat down, and placed her long, bony fingers on top of it. "My name is Agent Norton, and we have to work quickly. I know you are a smart girl. Smarter, I'm sure, than me," she said, and forced a laugh. "By now, you've probably realized the gravity of the situation that you've placed yourself in, and I hope you've come to the right conclusion."

The agent stared at Cody, as if waiting for her to speak. Cody didn't know what to say, so Agent Norton leaned in closer to her.

"We need your help, dear, and we need it now," she said. "Does that sound like something you can do?"

Cody thought for a second. She didn't really understand what this lady was talking about, but she saw no benefit in antagonizing her. Cody's only goal at this point was to leave as quickly as possible.

"How can I help?" she said.

Agent Norton smiled. "Good girl. I knew you were smart." She took out a pad and a pen. "Let's start with Kai Torres. Do you know where we can find him?"

Without having any intention of answering, Cody thought about where Kai might be at the moment. He surely didn't just go home after the school takeover. In fact, Cody couldn't even imagine that Kai had a home. He just seemed to appear and disappear on a whim. And wherever he was right now, there was a good chance James was with him. Of course, Cody wasn't going to answer that question.

"I don't know," she was able to say truthfully.

Agent Norton looked at her sternly. "Cody, I just pulled your phone records. I read all the texts. They were cute. But if you want me to help you out of this jam, you have to work with me. Now, what can you tell me about Kai's operation? What is he planning next? What do you know about the bombing?"

Cody pulled back, startled. She could believe that the authorities were interested in keeping tabs on the New Weathermen, but the way the agent was talking suggested something much more serious. It actually made sense, too. The more she thought about it, the more it seemed like Kai was a little more advanced than a college student who had taken up protesting just a few weeks prior. Still, if Kai had a secret life as some kind of super-spy, she hadn't been made privy to it yet. And there had been no discussion of a bomb.

"I really don't know what you're talking about. I'm sorry."

"All right, then. I can't tell if you're lying, but I guess we'll find out later, won't we? In the interest of time, though, I am going to offer you a get-out-of-jail-free card. It's not often you hear that meant literally, but if you answer this one question, and I mean really answer this in a way that makes me happy, that's how lucky I can make you. Do you understand what I'm saying?"

Cody nodded, her curiosity piqued. She was genuinely excited to hear the question that could carry so much weight.

"Okay, good," Agent Norton said, and stared her right in the eye. "What can you tell me about the Ark?"

The Ark. Cody sensed immediately that it was crucial to the Ones' fight. And much to her embarrassment, she hadn't the faintest clue what it was.

Cody shrugged, not wanting to give anything away. "Like I said, I don't know what you're talking about."

Agent Norton sat back, deflated, and shook her head. "God, I wish we could have done this the easy way. It would have been so much better for our friendship." She stared at Cody for an uncomfortably long time. For the first time all day and all night, Cody began to feel a kernel of fear.

Norton stood up from the table. "Cody, do you realize

that you are being held under the Equality Act? Do you know what that is?"

"Yes. It's an absurd law that allows the government to arrest and detain Ones indefinitely for any phony reason connected to terrorism. It's a law that violates the Constitution and hundreds of years of legal precedent. It's a law that disgraces our country. And it's also a law that doesn't apply to me. Because I'm not a One."

The past few hours had been so intense that Cody had almost forgotten what this whole fight was about. It wasn't just getting rid of a malicious high school principal. By reminding Cody about the Equality Act and the atmosphere that allowed it, Norton had refocused her and strengthened her resolve. She was here because her country was discriminating against its citizens. They were slowly crafting laws that normalized the subjugation of Ones. Someone had to stop this. That was why Cody was here.

Cody stood up defiantly to look Norton in the eye. "Now either tell me what stupid crime I committed at the school, or let me go. You can't keep me here forever."

Agent Norton smiled, as if something was dawning on her for the first time. "You're almost right about that. You see, the Equality Act was created as a tool to protect this nation in case the Ones ever began to pose a threat to the rest of the country. Kind of like they are doing right now. Luckily, we have a law that enables us to get a handle on them. To make sure they can't slip through some legal loophole and do some serious damage. The Equality Act also has a lot of fine print in it. And some of that fine print actually *does* apply to you, whether you're a One or not." Agent Norton began to recite from memory: "Any person engaged in a criminal association with genetically engineered individuals shall be subject to the provisions of this act in equal measure." She smiled at Cody. "Now, you wouldn't have anything to do with a group called the New Weathermen, would you?"

Cody had tensed up, not sure how much to believe. Was it true that she could really be held under the Equality Act even if she wasn't a One? She didn't think so. Kai hadn't seemed to think so back at the school. But she hadn't read every line of the law, now had she? That kernel of fear was growing.

"Whatever, so I talked to a One before. We still didn't commit a crime. You can't hold me for no reason."

"Didn't commit a crime? *We?* Cody, I don't think you understand. There's no one else. You're the only suspect. And I promise you, we can lock you away forever." Norton paused and gathered her belongings.

"You're being charged with murder."

=

Cody stood in a dark basement hallway and couldn't believe what she was seeing. On the other side of the thick glass window, a body lay motionless under a white sheet. Only the head was exposed. It was Margie.

Cody had seen her only hours earlier, when she'd checked in on the teachers before the SWAT team had crashed through the offices. She had even apologized to Margie for what Kai had forced her to do, staging the photo that depicted her about to hang from the light fixtures. Margie had reacted graciously, seeming to take a measure of enjoyment from all this unlikely excitement. She was invisible for most of her life, and then suddenly she was center stage during the most exciting thing that had ever happened in their town. And although Margie didn't actually say it, Cody suspected she supported what the students were doing, if only by virtue of the fact that anyone who had to work for Ms. Bixley probably wanted to get her fired, too.

But now Margie was dead. Cody could see her limp body laid out right in front of her.

Cody didn't understand how this had happened. Agent Norton, waiting in the hallway behind her, didn't offer an explanation. But Cody grasped how the facts were being laid out: The students took over the school. They publicly threatened to kill Margie. When the police arrived, Margie was dead. Cody knew none of them had harmed her, but it didn't matter. It certainly looked like they had. She closed her eyes and offered a prayer for Margie and her family. It was as heartfelt as it was pointless.

"I take it you believe me now?" Norton said from behind her.

"We didn't kill her. I promise you."

"Let's go." Norton grabbed her roughly and dragged her away from the morgue window. They started to walk briskly toward an exit.

"Where are we going?" Cody asked as they pushed through the door and into the cold air of the parking lot.

She never got an answer. Instead, as they stepped outside, a heavy black bag was pulled over her head. Cody heard a car screech to a stop in front of them and felt herself being lifted off her feet and thrown forward. She landed with a painful thud in what felt like the back of a van. A door slammed shut. The car started moving and didn't stop for a long time. Cody rode the entire way crying softly in total darkness.

=

The darkness followed Cody to her new home. It was a simple, square room. She measured it by pacing: three and a half strides in every direction, five strides on the diagonal. There was a door that fit perfectly in its frame without a shred of light on the edges. There was a slot in the door. A plate of food and some water was shoved through. Cody lunged at the food slot when she heard it open. It was the only way she could glimpse any light. Cody spent hours with her ear pressed to the door, trying to figure out where she was and what was in store for her. It was too cold to sleep, so she just sat there, shivering.

Finally, without warning, the door to her cell opened,

and someone stepped into the frame. Even with just the faint light from the hallway, Cody had to shield her eyes. But she could tell from the silhouette that it was Agent Norton. Cody's heart leaped with the promise of at least some new information. Anything this woman might reveal would be better than this silent treatment.

Norton stared at her and then pointed down the hallway with her finger.

"Let's go have another talk."

Cody jumped to her feet, eager to leave her cell before the offer was rescinded. Norton led her into an interrogation room much like the one at the police station. But Cody noticed that there was no camera in this one. She sat down on one side of the table and let her senses adjust to all the new stimuli. She could detect the scent of coffee from somewhere. And even though she hadn't seen a window yet, she could tell it was daytime. A few signs of normality. Cody couldn't resist a small smile.

"Beautiful morning, huh?" Norton said.

Cody nodded. "Can I go home now, please? I didn't kill Margie, I swear. I don't know what happened, but we never hurt anyone. Please, you have to believe me. "

Norton looked across at her, unmoved.

"When do I see my mother? And a lawyer?"

"Cody, you are a terrorist. We can do whatever we want to you. You will die in here." Cody began to cry. "Unless . . ."

Cody looked up, desperate, clinging to any sign of hope.

Norton continued. "Unless you help us. Do you under-stand what I'm saying?"

Cody nodded.

"You weren't very cooperative at the police station in Shasta. I hope you've had a chance to reconsider that choice. I know this hasn't been very pleasant, but I can make things better for you," Norton said, then paused. "And I can also make things worse." She opened up a note-pad. "So let's try this again, shall we?"

Cody listened to the same questions she had heard back in Shasta. They wanted to know about Kai, about the Weathermen, about any future operations. Cody tried to explain that she didn't know anything. It wasn't even a lie; she'd known them for only less than a week. Norton was obsessed with something called the Ark—clearly desper-ate for any shred of information about it—but Cody was utterly clueless and couldn't even help if she wanted to. And despite what she felt in her heart, Cody wished she had something small to tell them. She was getting the sense that it would be really bad if she didn't.

After not making any progress, Norton closed her note-pad. She looked up at Cody, disappointed. "I can see why Kai picked you. You're tough. And you're his type. But we'll get it out of you, won't we?" Norton stood up and left the room.

When she returned, Cody saw the bags for the first time. The clear bag was in Norton's right hand. The black bag was in her left. Norton looked down, contemplating the two.

"Water is always messier, but I think it's the best way to get our feet wet, so to speak," she said with a chuckle.

Norton moved quickly now, grabbing Cody's arms and handcuffing them behind the chair. Cody struggled to pull free but only managed to cut into her wrists. Then Norton grabbed the black bag—a canvas hood, really—and pulled it over Cody's head, the rough fabric scratching her face. Cody tried to shake it off, already struggling to breathe through the heavy canvas. Someone leaned her chair back.

And then the water hit her.

It fell on top of her in a heavy stream, and Cody managed to keep her mouth closed and avoid it for a moment. But the water kept coming, and Cody's shoulders were being held back and now she needed to breathe, but there was nowhere to turn for air. The water flooded the hood, making it tighter, sticking it to her face. And finally Cody had no choice but to open her mouth and try to get a gulp of air.

It was pure drowning. Even with her feet on dry land, Cody knew she was drowning. The water rushed into her lungs, filled her entire head, it seemed, and even as she gasped for air, all she got was more water. The pressure started to squeeze her brain, and her entire body began to burn, begging for oxygen. She thrashed and twisted as much as she could, but there was nowhere to hide. She felt the skin tear from her wrists and then her muscles spasm in desperation. The water kept coming. It poured into her body, and Cody knew it was killing her. She tried to scream but couldn't even make a sound.

And then, just as Cody felt like it was going to crush her, the water stopped, and someone pushed her shoulders forward. She heaved and gasped and spit and breathed all at once, finally feeling a trickle of air sneak into her body. It was the greatest feeling she'd ever experienced, this air that filled her lungs at the last possible second. She took another huge breath, ecstasy rushing through her brain with the oxygen.

The instant Cody relaxed, though, she was pushed backward again, and the water returned. As the onslaught filled her head and body, Cody began to understand the routine.

Drown, drown . . . breathe.

Drown, drown . . . breathe.

Drown, drown . . . breathe.

It went on like this for an hour, the waterboarding. Not torture, mind you, because the Equality Act didn't permit torture. It did, however, allow for enhanced interrogation techniques, which included waterboarding, as Agent Norton explained between dousings. Even from underneath the hood, Cody could feel her smiling.

And so it went, as Norton again and again brought

Cody to the psychological edge of death, all in the name of protecting the country from a group of principled teenagers.

Hours later, after she had been dragged soaking wet along the floor back to her cell, after she had lain motionless trying to breathe normally again, after she had sobbed and cursed and yelled and begged, after she had given up . . . some moment after that, a thought began to take hold inside her and lift her spirits.

She had been subjected to that for a reason.

No one could do that to another person without a good reason. No government could waterboard a sixteen-year-old girl without a good reason. Kai and the New Weathermen and whatever the Ark was . . . it was all somehow powerful enough to justify what they just did to her.

Cody, almost smiling now, began to realize that they did, in fact, have a good reason. They were scared.

CHAPTER 12

DEEP IN THE woods and many miles away from the school, James lashed out at Kai as they stared at the update on his phone.

"It says they have the suspect in custody. A sixteen-year-old student, not releasing her name." James paused for a second. "Cody is arrested for murder because of you!"

They had reached the area near the quarry, and Kai brushed past James and began poking around for a cavern entrance. James ran after him and got in his face.

"We didn't need your help. No one asked you to come to the school. And now Cody is screwed!" His words echoed off the limestone walls. As he continued glaring at Kai, James took a moment to allow himself a tiny sense of relief that at least she wasn't dead.

"Calm down, okay?" Kai said. "Obviously, she didn't

murder that teacher. When it all gets sorted out, she'll be fine."

James stared at Kai, heart racing but unsure what to do.

"And by the way, someone did ask me to come," Kai said. "Cody did. I know she said she didn't, but she was lying."

Taryn turned to Kai with a look of disgust. "Dude, what's the point of sharing that? Now you're just being an asshole."

"Oh, you too now? You're going to blame me for this also?" Kai said.

"No. But maybe we should be figuring out what to do instead of getting in a pissing contest."

"I thought you'd be happy. You clearly never trusted her," Kai said.

"Yeah, and now she's sitting in the room with God knows how many federal agents asking questions about us. I'd rather have her dead than in custody."

James looked at Taryn, taken aback. "What is wrong with you two? Seriously. Your answer to everything is to kill someone. As much as you want to believe it, that doesn't actually help our cause."

Kai shook his head condescendingly. "That right there is why we approached Cody, not you. No one asked you to get involved. In fact, why are you following us around? We don't need you."

James knew there was some truth to this, but he also

knew there was a part of him that Kai and Taryn hadn't seen yet. And now that Cody was gone, he was just as invested in this fight as they were.

"I'm not going anywhere until we figure out how to get Cody back. Shouldn't you have some brilliant contingency plan for that?"

"Who said we even want to get her back? If we couldn't trust her before, we definitely can't now that she may be cutting a deal with the feds," Taryn said, then turned to Kai. "Remember, she's not one of us."

"Cody will always be a One," James snapped. "You don't know her at all."

"Fine, let's say you're right and she tries to hold out. Everyone breaks eventually. They make sure of that," Taryn said.

James looked at Kai beseechingly. Even if they hated each other, James knew they at least agreed on one thing: Both of them had faith in Cody. They both knew how strong she was. Kai thought for a moment, clearly frustrated.

"There's not much we can do right now. I can talk to some lawyers we know, but if she's charged with murder, they're not going to let her out on bail. And if they think she's involved with the Weathermen . . ." Kai trailed off instead of painting a picture of what that would mean.

"That's exactly why you owe it to her to do something!" James exclaimed.

"We can't. It's too risky, and it's a distraction from our real objectives," Kai said. "One person is not worth putting everything else on hold. We all know there are risks involved in the choices we make. Cody knew that, too. We move forward without her."

And then to top it off, Taryn looked at James and chimed in to trap him. "That's what Cody would want, right?"

James couldn't believe how easily Kai and Taryn could rationalize this decision. They were colder than he had even suspected. It should have given him faith in their leadership, but at the moment it just guaranteed the miserable fate of the girl he loved. James couldn't stand it.

"If you're not going to help her, then I will."

James turned around, walked into a cavern, and disappeared into the mine.

=

He spent the night trying to sleep uncomfortably on the hard, damp ground. He had climbed as far from Kai and Taryn as he could, using the light from his phone, until the walls of the old mining tunnel narrowed too sharply. When faint traces of morning light trickled in from odd angles, James roused himself, found an exit hole, and re-emerged into the piney world of Mount Shasta. It seemed crazy to him how anxious he had felt being at the quarry just a week earlier. The stuff he was worried about then seemed so insignificant now. A little hazing from Marco was nothing compared with what Cody must be enduring. Without saying good-bye to Kai or Taryn, he started downhill and began the long trek home.

James needed the time to consider something serious. A nagging thought had kept him awake most of the night, but he still wasn't ready to accept it. The realization came at the end of one of James's typical logic sequences. He started with the basic problem: Cody was in jail, charged with a murder she didn't commit. James needed to get her out of jail. The Weathermen were of no help. James couldn't do it alone. It could probably be accomplished only by someone with more authority than the people detaining her. James needed the help of a government big shot. He didn't know any government big shots.

Unless . . .

This is where James hesitated. His gut told him that he did, in fact, know someone who fit this description, however much he didn't want to believe it. Still, James knew it might be Cody's only chance: He had to figure out what the hell was going on with his father.

What James had seen at the Cal State lab—a package from the NIH delivered by an armed guard—was enough to make him suspicious. His father was a normal college professor. He taught classes in the agriculture department. Sometimes he did research for the farming companies. But none of that should have connected him with the NIH. James had seen it with his own eyes, though, and had noticed how jumpy the package had made his dad. The NIH was the agency in charge of the Ones. Someone there might be exactly the type of person with the authority to help Cody. If his dad was doing something important enough, maybe he could call in a favor.

Something told James that this was a knot he didn't want to untangle. And as it stood now, he wasn't even sure of anything. He needed more information before he asked his father for help. He needed to go home and find out what kind of man his father really was.

=

When James got back to his house, there was a police officer in the living room waiting to talk to him. He looked exactly like the one who had chased him and Kai and Taryn across the campus. Even though he felt guilty, James tried to stay calm. With his parents looking on, the cop asked what James knew about Cody's plan.

"When did you know she was going to kill Ms. Morris?"

James tried not to laugh. He didn't want to antagonize the cop, so he explained it the best he could. "The *plan* was to have a peaceful protest and not harm a single person. You've got it all wrong. Cody didn't kill her."

James saw his mother shake her head in disappointment. "James, she's not worth protecting anymore. Just tell the officer what he needs to know," Helen said.

"Mom, stop it! She didn't do anything!"

"So you were there? You saw how she died?" The cop stared at him.

"Answer the question, James," his father said.

James wanted to protect Cody, but he knew lying and saying he was there would just make things worse. "No," he answered reluctantly, "I was in the library with everyone else."

The cop wrote something down. He asked a few more pointless questions, but James kept insisting he was just blindly following the crowd. The cop finally closed his notebook. "Every student who participated has been suspended from school indefinitely. And I've already explained to your parents: Don't go skipping town while we're still sorting this out, you understand?"

James nodded, and the cop left him to deal with his mom and dad. They each stared at him, shaking their heads almost imperceptibly.

"A woman died last night, James," his dad said, looking crestfallen. "And you played a part in that?"

His mom started crying.

"I had nothing to do with it," James said. That was true in a way. "And neither did Cody." Also mostly true, even if he couldn't explain exactly what had happened. "You know they'll do whatever it takes to blame this on the Ones. You don't actually believe them, right?"

Both his parents looked him in the eye but didn't answer. They stood up and left him alone in the living room. James was pissed that he had to defend himself to them, but he had bigger concerns at the moment.

On his way upstairs, he couldn't avoid a withering look from Michael, who clearly hadn't bought much of his story from the doorway where he had been eavesdropping. Maybe his parents hadn't, either, but Michael seemed angry about it.

"Just went along for the ride, huh?" Michael said.

"You heard me," James responded.

"Seems like you keep ending up in the wrong place at the wrong time. Maybe you should be a little more careful."

James had no interest in engaging with his brother right now. Still, he wanted Michael to know that he wasn't going to sit around and put up with all these Equality Movement provocations. James had proved that when they fought; now the rest of the Ones had done the same.

"You too. That nose still looks pretty messed up," James said, and walked right past Michael without looking at him. "Can never be too careful."

James kept a low profile in the house for the rest of the day and bided his time until everyone went to sleep. The wait was excruciating. Cody was in jail, and he needed to snoop around his father's life; it wasn't easy to sit still.

Finally, late into the night, when the house had been quiet for some time, James snuck downstairs and found his father's briefcase. He took his campus ID card and his key chain, which included some fancy device that flashed a unique seven-digit code every thirty seconds. James knew he would need that to get into the lab. Without making a sound, he trod softly out the door, got in his Jeep, let it roll quietly out of the driveway in neutral, and set off for the university.

James kept checking his mirrors, but he knew he was just being paranoid. He hadn't done anything wrong yet, and no one could possibly know what he was planning. Still, he felt the same surge of adrenaline that he had when they'd stormed the school office just yesterday. These two days were certainly outliers in James's orderly, obedient life. And this one struck him as even more unlikely because he was acting on his own. Cody wasn't cajoling him, Kai and Taryn weren't threatening him. He was breaking into his father's office because he knew he had to.

When he drove onto the campus, James parked in a lot far from his dad's lab building. He walked over there, barely seeing anyone but otherwise blending in to the college atmosphere. James used the ID tag to get into the science building. He nodded at a security guard who was half asleep at his desk and proceeded up a flight of stairs and down a long hallway. When he reached the office door with PROFESSOR LIVINGSTON written on it, James took out the keys and tried them until one worked. The door opened. James looked around and slipped inside. No one had seen him.

James didn't dare switch on a light, so he started looking around in the faint light from the streetlamps outside. He sat at his father's desk and tried to imagine where he would keep something important. He rifled through the drawers, but mostly he just saw student lab reports, lecture notes, and reams of test results about tomatoes. James knew he had to dig deeper, though. He was looking through every inch of a file cabinet when something struck him as weird about the middle drawer. It seemed to be shorter than the others, as if it didn't reach all the way to the back of the cabinet. James yanked the entire drawer out. Sure enough, it had been saving space for something.

The safe was small—about the size of a shoebox—and had a numerical touch pad. James tried to suppress his quick feeling of triumph. He stared at the touch pad for a while, contemplating how to proceed. He didn't want to start typing in an educated guess only to have the thing start hissing smoke at him. Or whatever angry safes were programmed to do.

James knew from other, less important passwords that his dad tended to use some version of James's or Michael's birthday. He thought about trying those eight digits, but he knew that if what was inside the safe was as important as he suspected, his dad wouldn't be repeating passwords that the family already knew. No, for something of this magnitude, his father would have chosen something even more meaningful. And then instantly, James knew what to guess.

His brother Thomas.

For his dad, losing his first son was the most impactful event in his life. That was what he would use to guard something so significant. As James leaned in to type Thomas's birthday into the keypad, another thought struck him. It wasn't Thomas's birthday that his father would fixate on; it was his death. James knew the date of his brother's death. It was a day of uncomfortable silence in his house every year. He typed it in, and the safe unlocked with a satisfying click.

Within seconds, James knew he had found something. There was a single folder in the safe, stuffed full of loose pages. The labels on the front cover were enough to give him shivers: TOP SECRET . . . NATIONAL INSTITUTES OF HEALTH . . . THE HOURGLASS VACCINE . . . ARTHUR LIVINGSTON . . . EYES ONLY.

James took the folder out of the safe, hands practically trembling under its theoretical weight. Just as he was about to open it and read its contents, he saw a shadow appear outside the office door. James lunged under the desk at the exact moment that he heard a key turn in the lock.

The door swung open and heavy footsteps entered the office.

James crawled as far as possible under the desk.

The faint lights from outside didn't reach him, so he knew he was concealed in total darkness. Even so, every breath rumbled in his ears. He put all his focus into holding the folder perfectly still. One crinkle of the papers would betray him.

The footsteps moved around the office, and a beam of light danced above the desk. James grimaced as he pictured the middle drawer left ajar in the file cabinet. He heard the footsteps stop there. The flashlight darted around with increased urgency.

And then, from under the desk, James could see two legs right in front of him. He drew back in surprise. This wasn't the regular campus security guard from downstairs, with his old-man orthotic shoes. No, this was an armed soldier in combat gear. The assault rifle that James had seen last week was dangling right in front of his face, the muzzle swaying gently like a hypnotist's charm.

The fact that a soldier was providing security for his father's office made James want to open the folder even more. If he got caught now, before taking a peek, he might never find out what was literally at his fingertips. But he didn't dare look. He held his breath and tried to stop his heart. Then James thought about what Kai had done to the cop who had chased them. Could James try something similar if he had to? He considered how much was at stake in this moment and resolved that he would have to try. James doubted it would be very successful, but he was too close to something important to go down without a fight.

Fortunately, he didn't have to take that chance. After hovering over the desk for a few more seconds, the soldier was apparently satisfied. He walked back out of the office and locked the door behind him. James waited for a minute, then crawled out from under the desk. He sat down, opened the folder, and started to leaf through it.

At first James couldn't really figure out what was going on. The papers seemed like all the other material in the office—charts and data related to some study that he didn't understand. But then James found a memo that was written in plain English.

He read it three times before he could believe it.

According to the memo, James's father, as an expert in the field of agricultural engineering, had been contracted to work on a secret government project. The project, taking place concurrently at various laboratories around the country, had one specific goal.

Find a way to reverse the genetic engineering of a living person.

James understood instantly what this meant. The government didn't just want to pass laws that persecuted the Ones. They wanted to eliminate the Ones altogether—they wanted to alter the very genetic material that made them Ones. Or as they would undoubtedly describe it, make things "equal" again.

He also understood exactly why his father would be so crucial to this far-fetched ambition. It was basically what he did already with fruits and vegetables. James shuddered as he thought about what was really going on in the lab down the hall. His dad was running experiments designed to create a vaccine that would transform every single One. A vaccine that would transform his own son.

James was overwhelmed. Fear, confusion, and anger battered his brain. And then he remembered why he had come there. To find something to leverage his father into helping Cody. Despite all those horrible emotions, he knew he had hit the jackpot.

James wanted to keep a piece of proof for the moment he confronted his father, so he slipped the memo into his pocket, then placed the rest of the folder back into the safe and locked it up. He put the office back into the condition he'd found it and leaned against the door, listening for the soldier. The hallway was silent. James slid out of the office, locked it, and tried to act like a normal college student walking through a science building in the middle of the night. Still, every few steps, he couldn't resist reaching into his pocket and feeling for that soul-shattering piece of paper.

Proof. Not just proof that his father was working with the government. Proof that Arthur really did regret that James had ever been born.

In a daze, James made it out of the science building,

quickened his pace, and walked to his car. He wanted to get home as quickly as possible. Confronting his father wasn't going to be easy, but he assumed that every second counted for Cody. He steered the Jeep away from campus and leaned into the accelerator. James didn't check his mirrors this time, so he didn't notice what else was on the road.

It was the single headlight of a motorcycle, far back in the distance, stalking his every turn.

CHAPTER 13

CODY HAD TRIED to measure time at the beginning, but it quickly proved impossible. Days and hours were the wrong terms. How could one keep track of time in a pitch-black room where nothing happened? Once in a while, Cody would feel tired enough to sleep. Did that mean a day had passed? Two? Or just a few hours that felt like forever? She imagined both of the extremes: Maybe she had only been locked inside for a very brief time that just felt much longer. Or maybe weeks and months were passing by in real time and she had no idea. Which was worse? Cody didn't know. It all felt the same.

Whatever a day meant now, Cody told herself to just get through it. Recite lyrics to every song she'd ever heard, go through the alphabet backward, do whatever it takes. Survive one more day in here, and something might change. She repeated it over and over: *You are always strong enough to get through one day.*

For all Cody knew, locked away as she was, the movement for the Ones had gained steam. Maybe the Equality Movement had their backs against the wall. Maybe Kai had wiped them all out. Maybe James had taken charge of a fair and honest government.

A girl could dream.

Even if it was a fantasy, it still emboldened Cody. And she did know one thing for certain: Until her last dying breath, she would not help any government that treated her like this. She cursed herself for wanting to cooperate on that first day, before the waterboarding had begun. Her selfishness disgusted her. No, she could never live with herself if she gave them the tiniest measure of help. It was settled—by virtue of their very behavior, they had ensured that Cody would never talk.

Cody delighted in their stupidity. Every day they kept her, every time they hurt her, she became even more determined to fight them. Cody felt these new muscles of hatred begin to build up inside her, and she was grateful that her tormentors kept exercising them. She knew she was getting stronger.

Even by the second time, dealing with the water was easier. Not just because Cody knew what to expect, but because there was no longer a debate in her own mind. Day after day, she was reminded of her options.

You are a terrorist.
We can do whatever we want to you.
You will die in here.
Unless . . .

Unless nothing. Cody shut off her mind and endured it.

Over and over and over again, she endured it. Sometimes the black bag and the water. Sometimes the clear bag and the suffocation. Cody endured it. Norton grew to hate her, became irate some days, screamed in her face. Cody endured it. They kept her in the pitch-black room and never let her glimpse the sky. Cody endured it.

They couldn't torture her forever, Cody realized. There was always, at the end of the session, the safety and comfort of her cell to return to. Her captors had families, other responsibilities, somewhere else to be. And when they left her alone, they didn't control her.

So Cody began to dream about the Ark. She had heard it mentioned so many times that it began to exist in her mind. There was nothing tangible about it, but she had a sense of what happened there. She played with her mother as a little girl. Her mom lifted her and held her to the sky and told her how special she was. The sunlight bounced off her eyes, and she scampered away joyfully, head held high. And James was there, too, leaning against a long shelf of library books, meeting her eye and grinning sheepishly. He would step toward her, slide his hand under her shirt, and run his fingers along her back. They would kiss. They would dance.

Was this the place that Norton so desperately wanted to know about? Was this the thing that threatened to destroy the world?

One day, when James was in her cell, she was so excited that she didn't know where to begin. She asked him if he knew about the Ark. She explained why she hadn't come home yet. She apologized for initiating the plan that killed Margie. James was nice. He didn't blame her. She reminded him about his promise if she ever fell into an eternal food coma. *You said you would live, James. You have to live. I might as well be in a coma forever. I'm gone.* James waved her off, but she insisted. And she thanked him for the way he had made her feel. *Before you came into my life, I stood out in every way . . . but I never felt special. You made me feel that for the first time. Absolutely special. You made me feel it every day, and you made me believe it was true.* James blushed. He didn't like talking like this. Cody didn't want to keep embarrassing him, so she let him off the hook. *I bet your mom still hates me, though.* They both laughed.

Other people came to visit her, too.

Margie came once, and Cody couldn't stop crying. She thanked her for all the candy she had taken over the years. She apologized, but she knew it wasn't enough. And she got the truth about the secret she'd suspected. *You hated her, too, didn't you?* Margie didn't answer, but her eyes said it all.

Of course, Ms. Bixley showed up shortly thereafter, her ears obviously burning. Cody didn't bother with any pleasantries. The instant she saw her, Cody stood up, knocked Ms. Bixley to the floor, and began to pummel her. She screamed at her, fists crashing down, hitting her with every ounce of strength. *You stupid bitch! I hate you! I hate you! I hate you!* Cody had a new relationship with violence now, but that didn't stop her from taking her rage out on Ms. Bixley. She beat her senseless and relished every second. Cody wasn't proud, but she still did it.

Her mother would come during the quietest times. Cody didn't have much to say to her; they had already talked before she went away. So they would just sit quietly, her mom taking her daughter's hand in her own, staring into the darkness together. It hadn't been easy, but Cody had come to terms with her mother's decision. *It's okay, Mom, I promise. I love you.* And then the truth that had been so hard to admit. *Thank you. Thank you for what you did for me.*

Cody was surprised when Kai arrived one day. She realized how little she actually knew about him. She wanted to learn more, to pry into his life, but she was still intimidated by him. Instead, Cody asked him about the Ark. He smiled proudly and told her she would have to wait. Cody was irate. *You still don't trust me? After all this time in here, and you still don't think I can keep a secret? I'm here because of you! I took over the school because of you! Margie is dead because of you!* Kai answered calmly. He didn't make her do any of that. She chose to stick with the Ones. And, he admitted, they were proud to have her. Cody wanted to stay angry, but even a tiny little compliment from him was enough to soften her. *Why do I even care what you think? What's so special about your validation that makes it so important to me?* Cody was genuinely curious and wanted to see how Kai would respond. He winked at her, and Cody hated him for it. Hated him because that only made it worse.

That was how the days piled up.

Torture.

Darkness.

Visitors.

Cody endured it. She grew stronger. She took solace in how afraid they were. She accepted that it might go on like this forever and she was helpless to change it. But she wasn't hopeless. She knew there was a chance that the world might be changing without her. That however unlikely it had seemed when she disappeared, maybe justice would prevail. Maybe Kai and James and all the other reasonable people would win the day, and then the maniacs in charge of this place would be forced to let her go.

Cody didn't think like this too often. It was too painful, like fantasizing about her favorite meal when she was starving. She pictured it sparingly, conjuring up the cheesiest, greasiest pizza and then illogically piling crisp salad on top, folding it up and shoveling it all down her throat. It was nice to imagine once in a while, when she really needed it, but for the most part, Cody denied herself the pleasure. It was silly to hope like that. Because nothing ever changed.

And then, one day, it did.

A visitor arrived who was actually real.

CHAPTER 14

JAMES HAD WALKED around with the memo in his pocket for several days, agonizing over what to do about it. He couldn't bring himself to confront his father, knowing full well their relationship would never be the same. On the other hand, Cody had been gone for a week now, and James knew he had to do anything in his power to bring her home.

He had gone over to her house to check in with her mother, and the reports were bleak: No one in the police department would tell Joanne where Cody was, and the lawyer she'd hired didn't fare any better.

"That information is protected under the Equality Act," they were told over and over.

James saw that Joanne was at her wit's end. She had tried everything, but Cody was in a black hole somewhere, and the conventional ways of getting her back clearly weren't going to work. If James had to play his trump card and blow up his relationship with his father, then so be it. Surely that wasn't as bad as whatever Cody was dealing with.

So he woke up early the next morning and waited for his father to come downstairs.

"I need you to do something for me," James said.

He could tell that his father was alarmed by his serious tone and direct request. James sat down at the table to signify that this was going to be a real conversation and tried to hide his trembling hands.

"I know about the Hourglass Vaccine. I know that you're working on it. I know that you've been lying to me."

"Son, I don't know what you think you've—"

James raised his hand to cut him off. "I am not here to debate with you. I just need you to do something."

"James, listen to me. You can't possibly understand what you're talking about. Whatever you think I've done, I promise there is a good, reasonable explanation. I can't tell you everything, but I can see you are confused. Now tell me what's going on, and we'll figure this out together."

But James just shook his head. He knew what the memo in his pocket said. And he wasn't going to let his father manipulate him.

"You need to get Cody out of prison," he said.

"What? How can I possibly do that?"

"You're going to call whoever you need to at the NIH, and you're going to insist on it. You're going to tell them that the secret work you're doing for them at the lab stops until she's free. It's that simple."

Arthur looked down, finally realizing the gravity of the situation. "James, it *isn't* that simple, I'm sorry. I can't just snap my fingers and set Cody free. What exactly do you think I am working on?"

"Dad, please stop lying to me."

"I'm not lying. I don't know where you heard this 'hourglass' word, but I don't know what you're talking about. There are dozens of projects that get worked on in the lab. Corporate, governmental, school-related . . . I can't keep track of every single one."

James was crushed. He had hoped that at least his father would be honest with him. That he would have some explanation for what James had found. Instead, James was forced to take the memo from his pocket and lay it on the table.

Arthur eyed it for a moment, shoulders sagging. "It's not what you think, James, I promise. Let me explain."

"Dad, do whatever you have to do—just get Cody back here. We can talk about what it means after that." James tried his best to remain stoic, but he could feel himself starting to cry.

"James . . ." his dad said tenderly.

"Dad! Just do it!"

Arthur was silent for a moment. "I might not be able to. It truly isn't that simple. One thing has nothing to do with the other."

"I'm sure there's a connection somewhere. However high up the ladder you need to go, that's what you'll do. Because I know one thing for sure: Whatever this Vaccine is, it has to be more important to them than Cody."

Arthur took a second to think. Then he nodded and looked James in the eye. "I will try. I will give it my best shot."

James could barely get his next words out. Even after he had discovered what his father was capable of, it felt so low to threaten him. But he knew he had to.

"There are crazy, dangerous people desperate to see the information on this memo. If you don't bring Cody home, that's who I'm giving it to."

James folded up the paper, put it back in his pocket, and walked out of the room.

James had nowhere to go. He wasn't allowed at school and was grounded by his parents, but he couldn't stay in the house after that, so he grabbed a coat and slipped outside. As he walked down to the street, he checked his pocket for the memo again. It was becoming a mindless habit, but he didn't want to let it out of his sight. And then, just as he reached his car, he saw Taryn sitting on the bumper, resting her legs on an old dirt bike propped up in front of her.

"Hey," she said.

"Hi," James said cautiously. "What are you doing here?"

"Jesus, good morning to you, too."

"Sorry, I just meant . . ." James had felt the need to apologize, but then he remembered where he stood with Taryn and Kai. They were refusing to help him with Cody, and Taryn had admitted to wishing her dead. So yeah, he didn't need to feel bad about being rude. "How'd you even know where I lived?"

"It's on a big list on the Internet, dummy, remember?"

Oh right, James thought. That was a fair point.

"The better question," she continued, "is why are you so jumpy?"

Taryn flicked her hand at James's face, not to hit him but just to make him flinch. He couldn't help it; he jumped backward and knocked her dirt bike off its kickstand. He tried to catch it, and Taryn leaped up to grab it, but it crashed to the ground. They bent down next to each other and lifted it up.

"I'm not jumpy," he said, not very convincingly.

"Well, sorry to catch you before your coffee, then. I just wanted to come by and apologize for the other night at the quarry. Kai was a jerk. I might have been one, too. We're supposed to be on the same side here, and we weren't so cool."

James looked at her warily, not sure if she was being serious. He knew Kai well enough by now to suspect that he may have put Taryn up to this. But she seemed like she was truly sincere.

"Thanks, I appreciate it. You guys aren't the easiest people to deal with, but I get it, we were all really stressed out."

"So no hard feelings? We can still work together?"

"Work together? I told you, I want to get Cody out. You didn't seem to think that was important."

"I know. I get why that's important to you. And I hope you see why we can't get involved. But I'm talking bigger picture . . . if we need your help, we can count on you? That *is* what Cody vouched for at the meeting, right?"

James didn't know exactly what she was asking, but he felt uncomfortable. He considered the New Weathermen dangerous, and he figured he should play along for now. He nodded at Taryn.

"Okay, cool. Just wanted to make sure," Taryn said, then hopped on her bike. "You're on permanent vacation, right? Maybe try and have some fun." She smiled, kicked into gear, and shot off, spraying James with gravel.

James got into his Jeep, feeling a little confused over what that conversation was really about. He just wanted to drive around and clear his head. Taryn being weird could wait—he was still trying to process what had just happened with his father. The clock was ticking on his ultimatum: Either his dad succeeded in bringing Cody home or James was turning the memo over to the New Weathermen. He didn't know if he'd actually be able to do that, but he hoped he wouldn't have to.

That was when James reached down to feel for the memo again. The only thing he felt, however, was an empty pocket. He shoved his whole hand around, disbelieving, but it was all too real—the memo was gone. As his panic threatened to explode through his temples, James fixated on two fresh, horrifying memories: the moment that Taryn bumped into him as they lifted her bike together and then the gleeful smile on her face as she rode away.

CHAPTER 15

CODY WAS LYING on the ground when she heard footsteps in the hallway. She darted, reflexively, into the far corner. If Norton was coming to take her to the other room, Cody always tried to delay it as long as possible. The corner was the closest thing she had to a safe haven. But when the door opened, it wasn't Norton standing there with the bags. Cody blinked from the light and tried to make out the larger figure. After a few moments, she had a flash of recognition. It made no sense, but the harder she looked, the more she believed it was true.

An arm reached out gently to her.

"Come on, Cody. Let's go home."

It was James's father.

Even as he placed his hand on her shoulder, Cody still wasn't sure it was real. She looked up into Arthur's face, saw a warmth she had never known from him, and let him help her off the floor of her cell.

"I'm taking you home, Cody. I promise," he said.

Arthur lifted her up, and before she could even comprehend what was happening, she was taking pained, tentative steps down the hallway, his hand on her back. No one else was around, and no one was stopping them. Cody wanted to run—she always did—but that was impossible for her body. So she pressed forward gingerly, each step making it seem more and more real: She was free.

Arthur's car was right outside. He helped her in, and then they were driving, through a security gate and onto a featureless road. Cody had no idea where she was, having only experienced these surroundings with a bag over her head on the floor of a van. After relishing the mundane beauty of everything she saw—sunlight, grass, clouds, a bird—she finally turned her attention to Arthur.

"Can you tell me what's going on?"

Arthur sighed. "Cody, it's very complicated. I'm sorry you were stuck there for so long. The only thing that's important now is that you're going home."

"Mr. Livingston . . . please," she said. "How is this possible? What did you do to get me out?"

"I really can't talk about it."

Then it occurred to Cody that maybe she wasn't going home. Maybe this was just the next step in her process of being dismantled. She had proved that the water and the bags wouldn't work, so they had devised this. Suddenly distraught, she saw that this new strategy was already working. It had only been ten minutes, but she had begun to feel hope again. Cody had given up in her cell, and that had made things much easier. Now, in an instant, she had something to lose. They were brilliant that way.

But why use James's father? Cody knew him well enough to know that he wasn't some elite government agent. And she truly believed that he wasn't a secret Equality Movement fanatic. So how was he connected to Norton and the people detaining her? Cody realized that regardless of whether he was friend or foe, she still couldn't answer the question.

Cody shrank back in her seat. Arthur saw this and reached out to touch her shoulder. She flinched instinctively and shut her eyes. Arthur pulled back as calmly as possible.

"I'm sorry. I didn't mean to scare you. But I promise you, Cody, I came here to help you. I promise to take you home."

Cody opened her eyes and looked at him suspiciously. She wanted to believe him, but none of it made sense.

"But . . . how?"

Arthur shook his head. He wasn't going to say any more.

"Just tell me one thing. Was it James? Is that why you came here?"

Arthur stared off down the road for a moment, then

finally nodded. And Cody remembered what love was again.

=

Hours later, several states later, and two incredible hamburger stops later, Cody finally believed it was real when Arthur pulled to a stop in front of her house. She got out of the car, walked gingerly to the front door, and pushed it open. Her mother obviously wasn't expecting her.

"Cody!" she screamed. "Oh my God, Cody, come here, baby!"

Joanne rushed over from the kitchen and embraced Cody so tightly that she could barely breathe. This was the good kind of not breathing, though—Cody had never before felt someone so soft and warm and welcoming. She held on tight, eyes closed, letting her mother try to squeeze their bodies into one. When her mother was done sobbing, she helped Cody to her bed, and Cody collapsed involuntarily before she could utter a word.

When Cody woke up, she felt the familiar panic of not knowing how much time had passed. She forgot that she could simply glance outside or check a clock to orient herself now. And even though it was her old bedroom, something seemed off. Cody shut her eyes to ward off the uncomfortable feeling, but her mom was at her bedside, and she reached out to take Cody's hand.

As Cody tried to calm herself down, her mom forced a steaming bowl of chicken soup on her. Cody took the soup and gave her mom's hand a squeeze. She knew her mom must have been absolutely shattered by the past few weeks, and she wanted to convey that they could both bounce back. Cody had caught a glimpse of herself in the mirror of Arthur's car, so she knew it didn't appear that way. There were bruises on her neck and blotches on her face. Her eyes were bloodshot and the hollows around them deeper. She barely recognized herself.

"It looks worse than it is, I promise," Cody said. She also took in her mother for the first time and noticed that she looked almost as bad. "Jeez, Mom, were they starving you, too?"

Joanne tried to smile but was still teary-eyed. "I was worried sick—can you blame me? They took my baby away and wouldn't tell me anything."

Cody nodded and pushed the soup back. She began to explain what had happened since the school takeover but left out the worst details. She didn't need to put her mother through any more pain. And more than that, she wasn't ready to relive them. Joanne explained to Cody everything that she had done to try to find her: the endless phone calls and days at the police station, meetings with lawyers, screaming in a federal courthouse. Nothing had worked to bring her daughter home. The Equality Act prevented that.

They both fell silent when they were forced to consider how James's father had managed to free her. It was still scary to think about, and neither of them wanted to unpack exactly what it meant. Joanne left her daughter to rest, and again Cody descended into a series of fever dreams. As she drifted in and out of sleep, she could hear voices coming from the rest of the house. James, definitely, pleading with her mother. Erica, some friends from the cross-country team, Mr. Oberlee ... Kai? She didn't know what was real and what was imagined.

As the days passed, she simply stayed home with her mother, trying to recover some sense of normality. And every night, in the darkest hour, she'd jump awake in terror, imagining footsteps coming down the hallway. Joanne would come in with breakfast in the morning and find Cody on the floor, curled up in the far corner.

Of course it was a relief to be home, but soon the joy of luxuriating in creature comforts was overpowered by a different emotion: anger. Cody began to leave the house with her mom, if only for a quick trip to the store or a walk in the park. The outings were brief, but Cody saw that things had only gotten worse since she'd been taken away. More Equality graffiti was showing up around town. Someone had hit the diner with a giant equal sign, sprayed in red paint. There were crazy headlines on the news racks. Harsher elements of the Equality Act were being enforced on the Ones. And in an odd twist, the person who accelerated all these events, Edith Vale, had apparently disappeared.

Prodded by these reminders, Cody began to fixate on

how badly she wanted to hurt the people who had hurt her. But she was better than them, and she wasn't interested in simply inflicting physical pain. Instead, she wanted to hurt them where it counted, by dismantling the entire apparatus that allowed her to be detained. She wanted to destroy the Equality Act. She wanted to destroy the entire Equality Movement. Before her capture, Cody's motives had been idealistic: She had believed in protecting the rights of the Ones and demonstrating to that end. But the torture had changed her. It had radicalized her, filled her with hatred, and created a more fearsome enemy. Now she wanted revenge.

Cody tossed and turned in her bed, fantasizing about getting back at Norton and the rest of the agents. She didn't know how she was going to do it, but she vowed to try. They were the ones who still kept her awake at night. They were the ones who had turned her into a hopeless, empty body. They were the ones who would have to pay.

After a few days of recovery, including a strict cell-phone blackout, Joanne let James in to see her. When Cody finally saw him in the flesh after countless hours of imagining his face, she felt a bit of a shock. He was almost too real: His curls were curlier, his nose even more of a button, his eyes a richer hazel brown. Cody wanted to leap into his arms, but she was still sore and moving slowly. And James clearly felt tentative, too. He inched forward into her room and stopped when he saw what she looked like.

"I'm not contagious," Cody said, smiling.

"I know," James said, embarrassed. "It's just hard to see you like this."

Cody waved him closer to her bed, sensitive to the fact that James was processing this reality for the first time. He knelt down next to her and reached out a hand to softly touch her face.

"My God, it's so good to see you," he said, eyes tearing up. Then he tried to laugh. "I think security is tighter here than wherever the hell you've been hiding."

Before he could say any more stupid things, Cody yanked his face down to hers, and they shared a kiss that she hadn't dared to let herself imagine when she was gone. It was pure bliss, a concept she had forgotten still existed in the world. Then Cody pulled James down onto the bed and snuggled under his arm. She lay there silently with him, gaining strength from the warmth of his body.

After what felt like an hour, she was at last ready to speak. "Can you explain what happened to me?"

"My dad says Margie had a heart attack when the SWAT team rushed in. When they found her dead, they framed you for murder and held you under the Equality Act for being a member of a terrorist group. After that . . . well, I guess you know the rest."

"Then how did I get out? How did your dad do that?"

James tried to smile at her. "Is that really important now? You're home. You're safe."

Cody pulled back from him. She wondered why he seemed hesitant to tell her. "James. It *is* important. To me. So tell me what happened."

"All right. I am kind of confused myself, but I'll explain what I know," James said. "When we couldn't find you or do anything for you, everyone started freaking out, trying to figure out ways to help you. My dad had an old friend from growing up—he's a lawyer in the Justice Department. He's not, like, the attorney general or anything, but he put my dad in contact with the people holding you. I don't know what he said, but I guess he convinced them to let you go. I'm sure they knew you didn't murder anyone, so I assume they probably would have given up eventually and done that anyway. You know, with or without my dad pestering them."

Cody couldn't help but laugh to herself.

You are a terrorist.

We can do whatever we want to you.

You will die in here.

They weren't just going to give up.

Cody didn't know if James actually believed this flimsy story or if he was the one hiding something.

"Wow," she said. "Good thing he had that friend."

"Yeah, really lucky."

"When we were driving home, though, your dad made it sound like you made it happen."

"Well, yeah. I mean, I was begging him to help. You

know, to think of something, figure out a way to find you. But it's not like I put a gun to his head or anything. He was happy to do it. I know you'll never believe it, but my parents actually do like you."

Cody decided to let James's explanation rest. "So what else did I miss? Any celebrities fall down naked or anything?"

"Yeah, like you care," James said. "I don't know if you saw yet, but schools all over the country had copycat take-overs. They weren't all successful, but it's obvious that young people are siding with the Ones. Of course, that's just making the jerks in the Equality Movement even more enraged."

"What are they doing now?"

James grabbed her computer. "You sure you're allowed to see this? Or is your mom going to kill me?" James opened the laptop, brought up a website, and tilted the screen toward Cody.

"Have you heard of an Equality Team?" he asked. She shook her head. "They are 'peacekeepers' with guns who are sent to hot spots around the country to enforce the Equality Act. They're everywhere now. They come in, intimidate the Ones into following all these new restrictions, and arrest anyone who doesn't comply."

"Have they been to Shasta?" Cody asked.

"Not yet. I guess we're not big enough."

James kept clicking through some news stories showing the recent interventions of Equality Teams, and Cody scanned the headlines: ONES SUBJECT TO NEW TRAVEL RESTRICTIONS . . . AGENTS CLASH WITH ONES DEFYING COLLEGE ENROLLMENT BAN . . . EQUALITY TEAM HONORED BY DIRECTOR NORTON IN D.C.

"Wait! Go back," Cody shouted.

James returned to the previous photo, and Cody confirmed what had caught her eye. It was a picture of a medal ceremony in Washington, D.C., where an Equality Team was being honored for bashing the most heads or something. And standing front and center, giving away the medals, was none other than Agent Norton.

Cody almost felt flattered. Her captor and interrogator was clearly someone important. She had sensed as much while she was detained, from the way Norton carried herself and the scope of her questioning. Norton didn't care at all about Margie's death. She was after something much bigger.

What is the Ark?

What is the Ark?

What is the Ark?

Now that Cody knew this for sure, her liberation at the hands of James's father made even less sense. What could Arthur have possibly offered to make Norton release her? Cody got the feeling that she might not want to know.

"What is it?" James asked, snapping her back to reality.

"Oh, nothing. I just can't believe some of these photos. They are really confronting people in the street like this?"

"Yeah. Gennycide. The whole country is cool with it."

Cody tried to wrap her mind around this new state of affairs. She wasn't surprised, but she was still saddened by it. And she realized she had played a part, however small, in creating this moment. She remembered that James had warned her against it.

"Just like you predicted," Cody said.

"Huh?"

"You said it a while ago. If we stay calm, this will blow over. If we act out, things will get worse. You were right."

"Well, doing nothing wasn't the answer. I came to terms with that when I was scraping gum off the floor. When we were segregated in our own school. When kids started getting killed because they were Ones."

"But I talked you into the school takeover, and look what happened."

"We have to be smart about it. That's what we were doing until Kai showed up. That's why you were taken away. It's the Weathermen that are the problem."

Cody knew some of this was probably true. But even though James had come around to taking action, he was still too many steps behind her. He wanted to continue with the peaceful protests. She wanted Norton dead.

Cody was the one who had been jailed and tortured. And what had he done to get her back? Asked his dad to make a phone call? As grateful as she had been to see him walk into the room, she'd never felt so far away.

She saw that James had picked up on that.

"What's wrong?" he asked.

Before Cody could answer, her door swung open and her mother stuck her head inside.

"Sweetie, you've got another friend who wants to say hi," Joanne said, then turned back to the hallway. "I'm sorry, I don't think we've met before...did you say Taryn?"

Cody jerked her head up, and sure enough, Taryn was standing in her doorway, holding a box of cupcakes. She looked totally different—nose ring gone, hair in a prim ponytail that must have been fake, muted clothes.

"Yes, thanks, Ms. Bell," she said in a bizarrely cheerful tone. And then she held out her arms to Cody. "Cupcake?"

Joanne left the room, and Taryn stepped inside. Cody saw her catch sight of James for the first time and noticed how Taryn stopped in her tracks. The two of them shared an uncomfortable look until James turned away.

"Oh," Taryn said. "I didn't realize it was a party."

"Not to be rude, but what are you doing here?" Cody asked.

"A girl can't come check on her friend?" Taryn said,

again with the odd Valley-girl affectation. Then she threw the cupcake box onto the bed and transformed back into her normal self. "You're being watched, Cody. Kai needs to talk to you, but he couldn't risk coming here. He knows they're looking for him. So he sent me. And we thought it might be better if I looked more like a basic Amber Reed clone than, you know, normal."

"I'm being watched? Did you actually see them?" Cody asked.

"Assume your entire life is under surveillance."

Cody leaned over to pull the curtains back and peek outside.

"So don't do things like that!" Taryn yelled, and bounded over to slap Cody's hand down.

James cleared his throat. "It's nice of you and Kai to check in on her. Kind of surprising, considering the last time you were talking about her."

Cody looked at James, confused.

"You can't trust them, Cody. All they care about is themselves."

Taryn looked at Cody. "Can we talk privately, please? It's him you can't trust—believe me."

Cody turned her head between James and Taryn. Even though there was still a gulf between her and James, she knew he always had her best interests at heart. She might not be able to count on him to help kill Norton, but she knew she could trust him to protect her.

"James can stay," she said to Taryn. "What do you need to tell me?"

Taryn glared at James, aggravated. Cody saw that she was choosing her words carefully. "The Weathermen want to debrief you, that's all. If you learned anything about what the Equality Agents are looking at, it would be helpful for us to know."

Cody thought about it and decided that this was a reasonable request. Not only did she want to help them, but she also had some questions of her own. An exchange of information would be very welcome.

"Okay. But if I am being watched so closely, how?"

"You like running, right?" Taryn asked. "Go out for a jog. Disappear in the hills. Tell us where to meet you."

"I don't think this is a good idea—" James started to say.

"Fine. I'll do it tomorrow. Right after sunrise," Cody said quickly.

"Where should I tell Kai to meet you?" Taryn asked.

Cody hesitated and looked over at James. She knew he didn't want her doing this. But that was a moot point now. The least she could do was not offend him by keeping it a secret from him. She turned back to Taryn.

"Take the Whiskey Meadow trailhead to the top, and keep going. I'll find him."

Taryn nodded and headed for the door. Cody saw her give James a withering look on the way out. The last time Cody had seen all of them had been during the school takeover. James and Taryn had always been tense around each other, but it seemed a lot worse now. Clearly something weird had happened in the aftermath, and she could tell James was keeping something from her. Cody wanted to ask him about it, but he stood up to leave.

"They used you and then threw you away like garbage, Cody," James said. "Make sure you remember that tomorrow." And then he walked out of her room.

Cody heard the front door shut and tried to consider what James was saying. She didn't really want to think about it, because she already knew she disagreed. She also already knew what she had to do.

So she started packing a bag.

＝

Cody knew it was cruel to be leaving again so soon, but she still slipped out of the house the next morning before dawn. The note she left on the table for her mother was brief but heartfelt. She hoped it was enough.

It felt amazing to be outside. She took several deep breaths of fresh air. Dawn was breaking, and the streets were quiet and empty. Cody jogged down the middle of her street, slower than usual, her wind gone, her legs heavy, and her backpack weighing her down. It reminded her, of course, of the day the Supreme Court had ruled against the Ones. But she wasn't anxious like she had been then. What was there to be afraid of anymore? The only thing left was to act.

Cody made it to the edge of town and found the trailhead that led up into the hills. As she turned onto it, James was standing in her path.

"James—" she started.

"Can I run with you?" he asked.

"James, you shouldn't have come." She saw him clock her bulging backpack even as she made a pointless effort to obscure it from him.

"Let me run with you. Please."

His eyes pleaded with her. She thought for a moment and then nodded. And as usual, she darted off ahead of him.

James caught up with her, and they fell into stride together. Cody wasn't laboring anymore. James's pace was pulling her forward, and she felt that exhilarating spring return to her legs. They ran in tandem, breathing as one, up the hills and through the trees. The sun began to creep through the lowest branches and warm their faces.

They were both beautiful, and the ground flew by underneath them.

By the time they'd reached the end of the trail miles later, Cody's mind had been on autopilot for so long that it was a genuine surprise to see Kai standing across the meadow in front of them, his face covered, as usual, by his dark hood. Cody slowed to a stop before they reached him and stood with James.

She thought about what awaited her on each side of the

meadow. She knew what existed between her and James: love, safety, familiarity. And she knew what made her pack a bag to leave with Kai: power, excitement, possibility. Cody selfishly wondered why those two extremes couldn't be combined, but she understood that this was impossible. The lack of one was inherent to the other. Neither she nor anyone else could ever have both, and she knew she'd have to pick. Cody wasn't ready to decide forever, but she was confident in what she needed now. She turned to give James a hug.

James started to talk, but Cody stopped him. "You don't understand what they did to me, James. And I care about you too much to make you share it with me. I know you—it would break your heart. So I have to leave. I have to handle this without you."

"Why?"

"Because I love you," she said. "I can't drag you down to the place I need to go. Even though I want to, it would be too cruel. Does that make any sense?"

James looked at her with tears in his eyes. "No."

"Then you have to trust me. Even if you don't understand, you still trust me, right?"

James nodded. "Always."

"You got me home. But my mind is still back there, and I need to fix that. When I do, I promise I'll come home for real."

Cody stood on her toes to kiss James on the lips. She

held him tight, even though he stood as still as a statue. And then, with each step harder than the last, she started walking across the meadow to Kai.

=

On their long hike to the quarry, Kai had the good sense to leave Cody alone with her thoughts. When they finally ducked through some thick brush and entered an old mining cavern, Cody was shocked at what she saw. It looked as if a college dorm had been set up in the tunnels, with fancy sleeping bags and laptops lying around in the dust. Cody recognized several of the Ones from the first meeting she had attended.

"There's been a lot of heat on us in the last week, so we just all started staying here," Kai said.

"What kind of heat?" Cody asked.

"The usual drunk Equality bozos. But more serious stuff, too. Cars following us. Our phones being hacked. Gunshots. Better to play it safe."

Kai didn't stop in this first area of the mine but continued leading her deeper underground into a smaller cavern, where they were alone. He stopped and turned to look at her for the first time.

"So . . . was it as bad as I imagine?" he asked.

Cody nodded. She had decided she would tell Kai everything. Unlike James, she knew it wouldn't hurt him. It would probably make him stronger, in fact. And since she needed his help now, she wanted him to know exactly what was motivating her. But before she got into it, Kai was ready to move on.

"I'm sorry you had to endure that," he said sincerely, then quickly switched gears. "Now tell me everything they know about us."

Cody suddenly realized this was a business meeting. Kai didn't want to check in on her as a friend; he wanted to pump her for information. She had to admit she was a little offended, even as she respected his professionalism—if you could call a militant student protester living underground a professional.

Most of all, though, Cody was pleased with how desperate Kai seemed for information. It meant she could make a trade.

"I'm happy to tell you everything I learned," she said. "But in exchange, I need to know something from you."

Kai nodded.

"What is the Ark?" she asked.

Kai's face immediately went blank. He didn't exactly reveal anything, but the effort he put into not having a reaction spoke volumes.

"Kai, what is it?" she pressed.

"I don't know. You tell me. Sounds like you know more than I do."

"I know it's important, Kai. They're scared of it. And I know you're involved."

"Cody, I have no idea what you're talking about, I promise. They could be messing with you for all we know."

Cody considered whether that could be true. Sure, they had been willing to do anything to shake her up, but Cody had seen the desperation in Norton's eyes. The Ark was real.

"Tell me, or I'm out of here," she said.

Kai stopped arguing with her and thought for a moment. "I get that you want to be looped in. And you deserve it. I wish I knew what you were asking about, but I don't. That's why it's so important for you to fill me in on every detail of what you heard."

Cody started to leave, but Kai reached out and grabbed her. She had forgotten how strong he was.

"Wait," he said. "There's something else I can tell you. Something you really should know. And trust me, it's big." He stared at Cody with those deep brown eyes. "Will that work?"

Cody could tell he was being serious. She nodded.

"Follow me."

Kai led them out of the cavern and even deeper into the mine. As he walked, he stared ahead, shining a flashlight and speaking without emotion.

"I'm sorry you have to hear this, Cody, but it's the truth. We've got the evidence to prove it." He paused and then laid it out for her in the simplest of terms. "The Vaccine is real. They are creating it on our campus. And James's father is the lead scientist."

Cody's mind accelerated into overdrive, trying to process what Kai had just said. Puzzle pieces started flying together, some of them making sense, others leading to greater confusion. But before she wrapped her mind around it, she realized that Kai was already way ahead of her. His strongest suspicions were a reality: The government was trying to re-engineer the Ones. He was capable of anything now. As they walked deeper and deeper, it was clear that Kai had already made up his mind about how to respond.

"What are you going to do?" she asked, not so much curious to hear his answer as genuinely terrified.

Kai didn't speak. Instead, he stopped in front of a hidden crevice and pulled an old wooden door out of the way. He yanked a tarp off a bulky pile at their feet. Cody squinted in the dim light to make out what was resting in front of her. Then she gasped.

Kai was making a bomb.

CHAPTER 16

IT WAS A long walk home for James. Ever the logician, he spent the entire time trying to understand why Cody had gone off with Kai. He could see that something had changed during her detention and that she had suffered more than he could imagine. Besides the physical toll that was obvious, her spirit for life had been diminished. But wouldn't that make her even more grateful that James had gotten her out? And what about everything that had preceded this month of their lives—did that not hold any weight?

He knew he wasn't really being fair to her. Of course Cody couldn't appreciate what James had done, because she didn't know what he had discovered to force his father's hand. He had debated telling her, first when she'd arrived home and then during their run through the hills.

James had sacrificed his relationship with his father for her. It was over for them now; there was no recovery from what he had found. If only Cody had known that, maybe she wouldn't have disappeared with Kai. But James knew he would have been forced to reveal the details, and those details were ugly.

The government was working to re-engineer the Ones.

Cody's paranoia was justified.

And his father was on the wrong team.

James realized that Cody might even blame him for this. And even worse, he knew that if he had shared this information with Cody, she would surely do something terrible.

James shuddered as he realized this was now a very real possibility. Taryn had lifted the memo from his pocket. There was no question that she had shared it with Kai. Would Kai share it with Cody? James wasn't sure. Kai was an opportunist; he would do whatever was best for him. Surely, at some point when he needed Cody's help, he would fill her in. James hoped that hadn't happened yet.

His thoughts turned to a more practical responsibility: Should he warn his father that the New Weathermen had evidence against him? Regardless of whether Kai had told Cody, the memo would surely prompt him to act on his own. James thought back to his brief experience at their meeting in the church and knew his dad's life was probably in danger. He had even threatened as much when he confronted his father, but James had never planned to actually give the memo to Kai and put his dad at risk. Now a more gnawing question sickened him to even think about.

Did James even want to save him?

He knew the answer to the question was no; the betrayal was too great. But he also knew his responsibility as a son, as a family member, and as a moral human being might require him to say something. James still didn't know what he was going to do when, to his surprise, he walked into his house and found his father waiting for him with a couple of tackle boxes at his feet.

"Get ready," Arthur said. "We're going fishing. Don't worry, I packed you a bag."

James would have thought he was joking, except his dad was wearing his old mesh fishing vest, the tiny pockets stuffed with different lures. Not exactly comfortable to drive in, but it definitely set a mood. And then his brother came down the stairs with a backpack slung over his shoulder, and James realized that a Livingston men's fishing trip was seriously being forced on him.

"I can't," James said. "You two go on without me—it's fine."

"You don't have a choice," Arthur said, and handed him a tackle box. He headed for the door and leaned in to James's ear. "Come on. We need to talk."

Arthur walked out to the car, and Michael followed

him, throwing another bag on top of James. "Shotgun," Michael said.

James started to accept that this trip was not optional. His dad wanted to resolve what had happened between them. James knew Michael was part of that, too. For all he knew, maybe they would jam a syringe into his heart and bring him home as a brain-dead zombie. But however unlikely it was, James still held out hope that his father could make things right. That somehow what James had discovered in the lab was all some big mistake. He knew it was childish to wish for that, to keep up the fantasy that his dad was some infallible, indestructible protector who never did anything wrong. Only six-year-olds thought that. In reality, fathers could be weak, petty, evil, and selfish. They didn't spend their entire lives lifting you up on their shoulders and letting your ice-cream cone drip down into their hair. That was what James thought of when he pictured him and his dad. He wondered if Arthur ever conjured up the same image when he was working on the Vaccine.

Apparently not, James decided. No one could have such conflicting thoughts at the same time.

James trudged out to the car, ready to hear what his father had to say. But as his father steered their car out of the driveway, he made it clear that James would have to wait a little longer.

"We have a lot to talk about, the three of us," Arthur said. "Let's wait until we're at the cabin."

They drove the three hours north in silence. The roads got narrower and the shadows from the pines grew longer, and James sat alone in the back, waiting to hear why his father was trying to transform him into an inferior version of his true self.

=

The cabin was basically an old mining shack that their family had spruced up a little over the years. It was a short walk to the Keswick River, where it was still a wide, lazy stream, well before the powerful rapids that rushed past Shasta. Up here you could belly flop off a rock and practically smother a dozen fat rainbow trout. Catching them on a hook was a different matter—one that involved a practiced alchemy of fly casting, timing, and impossible patience. Still, James and his family had made many successful hauls from the river, and even though the three of them had not gone out there together in a long time, he knew they'd have no trouble wading in, spacing out fifty feet from one another, and flicking beautiful casts into the shallows.

It was late afternoon now, and Arthur was looking James in the eye. "When I heard what they were planning, I was sick to my stomach," his father said.

They were sitting on stumps outside the cabin. A fire blazed in front of them, hissing and crackling sparks into the clear air. Arthur had asked James and Michael to come sit with him and listen.

"The highest levels of the government saw what was coming and needed a way to stop it. They didn't want to do anything ugly—anything violent—but they knew they couldn't allow things to continue on naturally. Inaction would lead to their extinction. Every one of us, of course, has an instinct for self-preservation. So they began a program to develop a vaccine."

James saw that his father had transformed into professor mode now. He was going to explain himself as clearly as possible.

"The original idea was to introduce a virus with a kill switch that would unravel all the previously engineered genetic material. But they couldn't get it to work right. The virus couldn't differentiate between organic genetic coding and DNA that had been manipulated. And even worse, would that really change the Ones in any meaningful way? Could it make a fully grown person become shorter? Turn their eyes from green to . . . gray? It didn't make any sense, and they realized that. So they threw up their hands and said, 'Well, if all these kids are too special for their own good, why not give them a handicap?' The next idea was for a virus that slightly inhibited every function of the brain. Reasoning, coordination, memory . . . everything. But when they started testing it, they couldn't calibrate it correctly. It was like using a bazooka instead of a scalpel, and the lab rats were waking up blind or paralyzed or not at all. That's when they called me."

Arthur paused, becoming a bit emotional. James saw that Michael was watching in rapt silence, which was understandable, considering that he was hearing all of this for the first time. To James, nothing his father had said was that surprising. He had already come to realize that the government was capable of such ill-conceived atrocities. What he wanted to know was why his dad agreed to help.

Arthur continued. "They knew from some of my previous work that I could scale a virus to work at just the right amplitude. 'Yeah, but on a vegetable,' I said. I told them I would never consider working on a project that would do this to people. And then I thought about it. I couldn't sleep for weeks. I knew they were pressing forward. I knew how bad their current version was—it was like a full chemical lobotomy. And I knew I could do better. So I decided I would figure out the safe, acceptable version of this. A vaccine that would satisfy them but not actually hurt anyone. Not actually hurt my own son."

James tried to make sense of what he was hearing. "So you agreed to work on the project to sabotage it?"

"If only that were possible. I knew that might work for a short period of time, but I couldn't impede it forever. There are dozens of other labs across the country working on it. I needed to come up with something real, as fast as possible, that they would still plausibly accept as solving the problem. So I convinced them that a fair handicap on the Ones would be a ten percent reduction in brain function. Comparable, I argued, to the advantage they had been given at birth. The NIH agreed that if I could devise a way to ensure this exact handicap, that would be an acceptable vaccine. So now do you see the position I was in? I could sit on my hands and watch them approve some barbaric, mind-numbing procedure, or I could help and steer them toward something more civilized."

Arthur looked to James, pleading for him to understand. But James refused to accept this binary excuse.

"Dad, you're acting like you had no other choice. Either do nothing or work for them. What about a third option, the obvious one? Try to stop this whole thing from happening! Scream from the rooftops! Warn people! Did you ever consider that?" James yelled.

"It's easy to say that, but there was no way to stop it. I would have been silenced. That means *killed*, James. So I tried to find a solution I could live with. And let's remember, somewhere in this technology, there is the power to make miracles. To end birth defects. To abolish genetic diseases. To prevent an immeasurable amount of human suffering. We are morally compelled to do that if we know how."

"And what about me?" James asked, incredulous. "Am I supposed to rush down to the lab to get 'handicapped' by ten percent? What the hell does that even mean? Why should I be changed at all? I didn't do anything wrong! Forcing me to change one hair on my head is too much. It's not fair."

"James, it is unfair. Life is unfair. But most of all, this mind-blowing idea of engineering our babies is unfair. *You* are unfair. I know it's not your fault, but we messed up. This country messed up. Your mother and I messed up. I came to realize that as I watched you and your brother grow up. I wish I could have undone it. And then, when the government wanted to do something much worse, I saw that I could. In a dignified and measured way. I could fix our family."

James believed that his father's heart had been in the right place. But it was still hard to accept that he wanted to change James, to alter the identity of his own son. The anger from that would not go away.

Michael reached out to put a hand on Arthur's shoulder and spoke for the first time. "I think you did the right thing," he said, then turned to James. "He was trying to protect you. And to help us. You can't hold that against him."

"We are not guinea pigs, Michael. You can't just mess around with who we are—I don't care how *dignified* it is."

Michael laughed. "James, you are a guinea pig. A science experiment gone wrong. You must know that, right? Dad is trying to fix this for you in the best way possible. If you can't accept that and forgive him, then good riddance. Don't bother being a part of this family anymore."

Michael stood up and walked away from the fire. James turned to check his father's reaction. He stared off after Michael dejectedly.

"A long way to go, I see," Arthur said, then paused for a moment. He and James stared into the fire. "Look, James, please don't listen to that ultimatum about leaving the family. Of course that's not true. But I really do hope you think about what I was trying to do. And I hope you can forgive me. I am proud to call you my son. I love you. And I will always love you, no matter what you think of me."

Arthur stood up and was about to leave James alone by the fire. But he stopped, knelt down next to him, and leaned into his ear.

"I would have never given you the shot. I would have made sure you had a placebo. As long as Michael believed it was real, that was the only thing that was important. I could never actually do that to you."

James felt tears well up in his eyes. This was the father he so desperately wanted to believe still existed. Not the evil scientist but the loving genius who would let him drip ice cream into his hair. A wave of relief flooded his brain. And then a question.

"When you gave me the placebo vaccine . . . would you have told me it was fake?"

Arthur smiled at James. "Would I have needed to?" And then he walked away.

≡

They were in the river early the next morning, all three of them, spaced out at just the perfect distance that made it impossible to talk. James lazily cast his fly back and forth, but he wasn't thinking about catching fish; he was trying to process what his father had said the night before. Even if it was exactly what he'd wanted to hear, James still had some reservations. For one, it was a little too convenient. And more important, there was no way to prove that his father wasn't still lying. His claim that he never would have administered the Vaccine to James sounded great, but it was about a hypothetical moment in the future. And what about everyone else?

As James thought about it more deeply, though, he decided that his father deserved the benefit of the doubt. For seventeen years, he had done nothing but look out for James. And it hadn't been that easy, with Michael always resenting him and his mother still holding a torch for Thomas. His father was smart. He understood that the rise of the Equality Movement meant that there was no chance for a perfect resolution to the Ones controversy. So he had inserted himself into the problem to protect James the best he could. Maybe it all made sense.

James knew the ball was in his court. He had to confess that he had lost the memo and warn his father.

Whatever Kai was planning to do, James had to help his father stay safe. And when they got back to Shasta, James could try to convince Kai that his father wasn't the real enemy. That would be a tough sell, obviously. Maybe his father would have to do that himself. Look Kai in the eye. Explain how he got Cody back. And justify the horrifying project being run in his laboratory.

James considered the best way to make this all happen. It was delicate but possible. He looked down the river at Michael and his father. The sun was high above them now, perfect for a shadowless cast. His father looked up and waved. After a moment, Michael nodded at him. For the first time in years, James felt a thread of hope running through his family.

As James tried to relish the rare moment of bonding, their quiet stretch of the river was interrupted by a loud shout.

"Ahoy, sailors!" came a cry from the tree line.

James, Michael, and Arthur looked up and squinted into the woods. Two hunters waddled down to the river-bank. They were laden with two powerful rifles and enough blaze-orange clothing that James almost had to avert his eyes.

"Fish running good?" one of them shouted.

Arthur nodded politely. "No complaints. Good luck with the deer." He cast another fly.

But the hunters came down to the water's edge. One of

them knelt down and splashed his hand around. "Yup, feels about right," he said. "Say, you fellas mind looking at this map for a second? Me and Dale kinda lost the scent, so to speak."

Arthur reeled in his line and sloshed over to the hunters. Michael followed, and James joined them. The first hunter, who was tall and gangly, opened a map, while the second one took out a flask and tilted it up to the sky. Then he offered it to Michael and James.

"No thanks," Michael said. He nodded admiringly at the hunter's rifle. "You guys going after bucks?"

"Shit, I haven't even been looking. I just came to walk around outside and get drunk."

The first hunter slapped his friend with the map. "Shut up, Dale." He turned to Arthur. "He ain't much of a woodsman."

"No, but I like shooting shit. Damn, Willis, when we gonna shoot at something?" He wheeled around with one hand on his rifle, and James jumped back.

"Soon as you stop scaring everything but the flies away."

"Ask 'em where the deer are," Dale said, nodding for Arthur to look at the map, then taking another nip from his flask. "Shit, ask him were the gennies are hiding."

"I said shut up, Dale!" Willis snapped.

James and Michael exchanged a tense look.

"What? What'd I do? You can ask them," he said, and turned to Arthur. "We heard some gennies were hiding out in the woods, making plans and whatnot. It ain't just deer season, am I right?" He held his gaze on Arthur and offered him the flask. By the way he gestured, it was clear he was insisting. Arthur hesitated for a second and then took a sip.

"We haven't heard a peep. Just some quiet family time with my boys," Arthur said.

The drunken hunter turned his gaze to James and Michael. He cocked his head and narrowed his eyes. Then he jabbed his buddy with the tip of his rifle and gestured with it at James and Michael.

"Shit, Willis, look at these two. Damn near cut from granite, huh?" He swung his arm hard against James's shoulder. "Ouch!" he yelled, shaking his hand, exaggerating.

Willis stepped over and looked at James and Michael. He turned to Arthur and grew serious. "You sure you haven't seen anything?"

Dale leaned into James's face. "I swear, this one is pretty enough to kiss."

James felt the man's warm breath in his nose and lifted his arm against the hunter's chest, just to get some space. The other hunter wheeled on him and leveled his rifle.

"Watch it there, boy."

Arthur tried to step between everyone. "All right, gentlemen, let's just all take it easy. Please stop pointing your rifle at my son."

Dale hopped around with excitement. "We found some, Willis, I told you!"

"These are my sons. We came out here to fish. You might be looking for trouble, but we're not."

The tall hunter held his gun steady. "These are your kids, huh? Don't you lie now . . . are they gennies or not?"

Dale reached out and pinched both James and Michael on their cheeks. "Just look at them!"

Arthur stepped forward and smacked the hunter's arm down. "Get your hands off my boys!"

The other hunter turned his rifle to Arthur. "Hey!"

But James's father didn't budge. "How dare you! I know how these boys were made." Then, to James's shock, Arthur grabbed his crotch with a flourish of pride. "They were made the old-fashioned American way." The hunters stared at Arthur. He stared back defiantly. "No kid of mine is a fucking genny."

There was a moment when the only sound was the water rippling onto the bank. And then, in an instant, the hunters both started laughing, tilting their heads back and cackling up at the sky.

The tall one patted Arthur on the back. "Sorry, pal," he said, then turned to his friend. "Damn it, Dale, quit molesting and offer them a drink, for Chrissake!"

James watched as Arthur smiled back at the hunters. He knew, of course, what his father was doing. He was keeping them safe. But even good intentions couldn't

235

mask a deeper, more important truth: His father truly didn't have the heart to stick up for him.

This sudden and bitter realization finally settled it for James: He couldn't bring himself to warn his father about Kai.

CHAPTER 17

CODY LAY AWAKE the whole night. For starters, Kai had thrown his sleeping bag down right next to her. He had passed out quickly, but Cody could feel the warmth emanating from him. The mine was drafty, and as she tossed and turned, she couldn't help but edge closer into the cozy shelter that his body created. But even when she got warm, her mind wouldn't stop racing.

The Vaccine.

James's father.

Kai's bomb.

Cody tried to tackle them one at a time, but they were all so interconnected now. James's dad made the Vaccine, so Kai made a bomb. After what she had already endured, Cody thought she could handle anything. She was prepared to die to fight back against the Equality Movement. She would resort to any measure to have her revenge on Agent Norton. But this—this wasn't as simple.

Of course now Cody understood how Arthur had gotten her released from detention. But even after Kai had shown her the memo, she still had trouble believing it. Arthur was so wise and reasonable, just an older version of James. And his own son was a One! The idiots who spray-painted equal signs were one thing, but how could Arthur have sat with his family every night after working all day to destroy them? That was a different kind of monster.

Cody thought back to their first moments driving away from her prison, when she had asked if he was doing this for James. Was it a gift to his son, or did James force him? If James had forced him, then James knew about the Vaccine. And it meant that James had used that leverage not to destroy the program but to save her.

She hated him and loved him for that.

Now it was her turn. She had to choose between fighting against this evil or protecting James—or in this case, his family. James had picked her. In the brief time she had to contemplate, Cody knew she couldn't return the favor.

The Vaccine was too big. No person deserved to be changed or diminished at the behest of the government. Cody knew she wasn't in danger from it, but the rest of the Ones were. They were all just kids, essentially, ranging from babies to college students. It was hard enough figuring out who you were without scientists prying into your genes and crossing the wires. That is, after you were alive already. Cody didn't care who was in charge or how much she might owe them—she knew she had to help stop it.

Still, her heart broke picturing her mother waking up to find her daughter gone again, but Cody hoped she'd understand. Her mom would have read the note a dozen times since she'd found it that morning. Cody had tried to strike a tone of optimism, even if she knew there was a chance she'd never return. And she ended it with a declaration that she knew her mom needed to hear: *I know exactly who I am . . . proud, stubborn, idealistic—in other words, YOUR daughter—and I wouldn't change a thing.*

Now, as she tossed and turned in the mine, Cody's thoughts turned back to the pile of fertilizer and chemicals that Kai had unveiled. It was all jumbled together in a large suitcase, with wires running through it. Following the science, Cody knew how it would work, understood exactly how the ammonium nitrate in the innocent-looking mulch would vaporize upon detonation and release oxygen that would feed the subsequent explosion. She knew it was a weapon of powerful violence, and she couldn't help but feel a wave of excitement just looking at it. This was why she had come to Kai and the New Weathermen. This was how she was going to get her revenge.

Cody didn't feel any guilt for this instinct. Instead, she thought back to what her captors had put her through. First the fear, then the pain, and then the hopelessness. The smiles as they tried to kill her. The taste of the airless plastic bag. The room they had left her to rot in, dark and freezing. The way the walls seemed to close in on her every day and the air would get sucked out, and how she thought she'd suffocate not with her head in a bag but by clawing at the steel door, blood running from her fingertips and down her arms in dark, desperate streaks.

Cody sat up and tried to shake herself out of the flashback. She knew she wasn't back there, but as she looked around, all she could see was darkness. The tunnel felt narrow and on the verge of collapse. A cold draft blew up from the depths of the mine. She felt around for her flashlight and couldn't find it. She gasped for air, struggling to breathe. She had to get out.

With arms extended, Cody felt her way along the tunnel, scraping her hands and face and tripping with every other step. But it was too tight in there—she had to get above ground—so she raced forward blindly, hugging the wall, crying, and growing light-headed.

At last, she felt a change in the air and smelled the pine needles. A few more steps and moonlight trickled in from the mouth of a tunnel. Cody lunged out of the mine and collapsed on the ground, the stars above finally proving she wasn't trapped. As she took deep breaths and regained her senses, her hatred for the people who still tormented her hardened even further. They had left her like this: an angry, broken shell. She was ready to blow things up because of them.

But a spark of humanity still burned deep within her. She knew she would still be locked away were it not for one man. Whatever else he had done, she owed her life to that man. Cody couldn't bring herself to kill James's father.

=

Cody woke up in the mouth of a mine tunnel with Kai kicking her feet. He tossed her an apple and started walking away.

"A sleepwalker, huh?" he said. "Come on, we're already behind schedule."

Kai stepped back into the mine as Cody blinked awake. She stood up, dusted herself off, and hesitated in the entrance. She had wanted to talk to Kai about the bombing, to volunteer her support, but only on certain conditions. Of course Kai was already walking briskly away, so she had no choice but to chase after him. It was impossible to ever talk to him on her terms.

Cody caught up with him just as he ducked into a side tunnel. He stopped at the same wooden door she had seen the night before. Kai stepped through the crevice, and a moment later Cody followed him into the bomb room.

Besides Kai and the bomb, there were two other people: Taryn, who flashed with anger as she stepped in, and Brandon, the One from the first meeting who Cody remembered was a real stickler for the rules.

"Hell no," Taryn said to Kai. "She's not coming."

Brandon threw his hands in the air. "Kai, you're kidding, right?"

"We need four people," Kai said. "She deserves to be there. She's earned it."

"Kai, you said you needed to bring her here to debrief her. But she's not even a One—she could ruin it for all of us. No," Taryn said.

Cody decided to speak up. "Who said I even wanted to come?"

"Perfect, she's not up for it. Then it's settled," Brandon said.

Kai turned to her, incredulous. "We can get into the lab that's creating the Vaccine and blow it to the sky, and you don't want in?"

"I didn't say that. How about you tell me the plan before anyone makes a decision for me?" Cody said.

"You see that?" Taryn asked, pointing at the covered tarp in the middle of the floor. "It goes *boom*. Now see you later."

Kai stood up and pulled the tarp back, revealing the bomb materials. "We built it for the Christmas-tree lighting. It's got a blast radius of three hundred yards. Four hundred pounds of fertilizer, ammonium nitrate, and gasoline." He glared at Taryn and Brandon. "That's why

242

we need four people." Kai brushed some dust off the wires delicately, almost lovingly. He turned back to Cody. "But once we found out about the chemistry lab, changing the target was a no-brainer. She's beautiful, isn't she?"

Even in her jittery excitement, Cody couldn't get past something Kai had just said. "You were going to blow this up at the Christmas ceremony? With the whole town there?" Even in her state of rage at the Equality Movement, Cody didn't understand how such a murderous act would make sense.

"Don't worry about that now, Cody," Kai said. "We know where the Vaccine is. That's all that matters."

These people clearly didn't care who died as long as it made a statement. Cody suddenly realized what she had signed up for and decided to choose her words carefully. "I want to stop the Vaccine more than anyone. But I can't kill Arthur Livingston. I owe him my life."

Cody saw Taryn shoot a look toward Kai. But Kai didn't seem worried. "That's fair," he said. "We don't care about killing him, anyway. We're doing it at night—no victims— This is going to be a statement about the Vaccine, not an assassination."

"So James's dad is safe?" Cody asked.

"Sure. We can deal with him later if we need to, but that's not what this is about. You have my word."

Kai and the others stared at her, waiting for an answer. Cody didn't need to hesitate; it was pretty clear-cut for her now. The Weathermen had found out where the Vaccine was being developed. They had constructed a bomb to destroy it. And they had agreed to spare James's father. Cody hated the idea of Kai "taking care" of him later, but if Arthur decided to keep working on the Vaccine again, she wasn't sure she could save him, or even if she should.

"I'm in." She looked around and stared everyone in the eye. They all nodded.

"We still have some prep work to take care of," Kai said. "If it all checks out, we plant the bomb next Wednesday."

There was a knock on the wooden door concealing their crevice. As Taryn rushed to pull the tarp back over the bomb materials, a voice called out from the other side.

"Kai, you really need to come see this." It was Daphne, one of the other Weathermen Cody had seen when she arrived.

"Not now."

"I promise you, it can't wait," Daphne said.

Kai pulled the door back and stepped into the tunnel. Cody and the others followed Daphne back to the top of the mine, where the Weathermen had set up their base camp. Everyone was huddled around a laptop with a thick cellular antenna. They were watching a live news report.

Cody immediately recoiled as she saw Agent Norton's face speaking into the camera.

"As the head of the FBI office entrusted with keeping

our country safe, I've asked an emergency session of Congress to pass this law immediately. The new protocol will ensure that this recent wave of violence comes to an end and will allow us to handle the pressing issue of our genetically engineered citizens in a more organized and productive manner."

"What is she talking about? What is the new law?" Cody asked in a panic.

"I ask all of the people affected by this law to report to their new residential camps as quickly and peacefully as possible. This is for your own safety. Parents, please help them. After the law passes, if you're not already at your designated camp, the federal marshals on our Equality Teams will escort you there. Thank you, and God bless America."

Agent Norton stepped away from the lectern, and the Ones all looked at each other in shock.

"They are shipping us to internment camps," Daphne said. "Congress is having an emergency session later today. Apparently, the camps are already set up, and the buses are on the road."

Cody tried to imagine how this was possible. Her government was preparing to take one percent of its children and force them into a camp. To steal their lives away from them. To banish them. And then it dawned on Cody what would actually happen to the Ones at these camps. As she realized it, Kai was already saying it out loud.

"They're ready to give us the Vaccine." He stepped back

from the group and began heading down into the mine. "Change of plans. We plant the bomb tonight."

≡

Six hours later, as the last sunlight slanted through the trees, Cody carried her share of the bomb's weight away from the mine. She walked in step with Kai, Taryn, and Brandon, each of them holding a corner of the heavy suitcase on their shoulders and struggling over the uneven terrain. They looked like pallbearers.

A few hundred yards away, Kai had parked an old van at the end of the dirt road that led to the quarry. They opened the doors and gingerly slid the suitcase into the back of the van. No one wanted to give it the slightest jostle. When it was strapped down securely, Kai climbed into the driver's seat, and Taryn took shotgun. Cody had already noticed that she had her pistol tucked into the back of her pants. Before she hopped into the back to join Brandon, Cody considered what she was getting herself into. She imagined what the worst-case scenario might be and realized she felt like she had already endured it. Surely, though, she wouldn't get so lucky a second time if they were caught tonight. Rushing like this was only going to increase those chances. But Cody agreed with Kai: After the announcement that Norton had just made, they needed to act fast. These might be the final few hours when Ones would be able to move around freely. Cody got in the van and shut the back doors behind her.

They started driving down the slope of Mount Shasta, the racing van keeping time with their adrenaline. After a long period of silence, Brandon finally brought it up.

"Kai, we might not be ready to do this. I mean, the plan we made for next week . . . it only works if we do it next week. The guard schedules, the night technicians . . . even if we can make our way in, it might not be empty tonight."

"We'll see what's up when we get there and figure it out," Kai said.

"Brandon might be right," Taryn said. "There's no point if we can't—"

"I said we'll figure it out!" Kai bellowed. He pressed down on the accelerator and tightened his grip on the steering wheel. "We don't have a choice, okay? It's now or never. Tonight or the camps. The plan stays the same. Brandon still has the entry code. If there's a guard, we take him out. I don't care how hard it is, we are blowing up that lab tonight and destroying as much of the Vaccine as possible."

The matter seemed settled, but Cody knew she had to speak up. "As long as James's father isn't there."

Kai looked into the rearview mirror and met Cody's eyes. He stared at her for a long moment, his wild energy barely able to contain itself. He held her gaze, then finally answered.

"Right. That, too."

Then Taryn tapped him on the leg and gestured through the windshield.

"Watch out," she said. They had come to an intersection at the base of the mountain, and a police car had pulled up to a stop sign directly across from them.

Cody felt a cold sweat cover her body. She stared across the road and saw the cop eyeing them. This was someone who could send her right back to the dark, cold corner of her cell. He would only have to glance inside their van.

All four of them held perfectly still as the cars faced each other. They probably would have sat like that forever had the cop not raised his arm and waved for them to come forward—he was gesturing them through the intersection.

Kai steered the van straight ahead, and they passed by the police car with barely a glance from the cop. Cody finally exhaled and collapsed back against the wall. Kai looked back and smiled at her. He reached out to touch the suitcase.

"That would have been one hell of a ticket," he said, laughing. Everyone else couldn't help but smile. Then they rode the rest of the way to the lab in silence.

⸗

They waited for the perfect hour: late enough for the campus to be quiet but not too late to draw suspicion while walking around. Brandon got out of the van a few blocks away from the science building. He needed to use the lab for a chemistry class he was taking that semester, and his student ID was programmed to give him access. He would go first and let the others into the main area. Taryn hopped in the back of the van and showed Cody a schematic drawing of the building. Adjacent to the lab was a locked room that only Professor Livingston had the code for. That was where they wanted to put the bomb, but they couldn't figure out a way in. Kai had come up with a simple work-around: Make the bomb so damn big that it didn't matter. If they left it pressed against that door and everything went as expected, the room with the Vaccine would be obliterated. The bomb had a cell-phone-activated detonator that they would call from the car.

They waited for Brandon to gain entry, then pulled the van closer to the building and stepped outside. Taryn popped open the back doors, and the three of them struggled to pull the suitcase out. They got it on the ground, wheels on the bottom. It would be heavy to roll, but it was better than lugging it through the forest.

Kai took the point and walked ahead. Taryn followed at a twenty-pace distance, rolling the suitcase behind her. Cody brought up the rear, another twenty paces behind Taryn. They approached the entrance to the building.

One after another, they swiped in with student IDs, Cody using a card borrowed from Daphne. The campus security guard in the building barely looked up.

Kai took the stairs, Taryn pressed a button for the

elevator, and Cody joined her. They took it to the second floor and emerged into a bright, clean hallway.

Rounding a corner, Cody saw that Kai was approaching an armed soldier sitting in front of the lab door. Kai, his posture oddly crooked, had a ratty backpack slung over one shoulder, and he was holding a notebook open as he walked up to the soldier. Kai got very close to him, and the soldier lifted his arm to maintain some personal space. His heavy assault rifle hung off one shoulder, just like Kai's backpack, and Cody was struck by the odd similarity. Then, in a blur of motion, she saw Kai pull something from his own back pocket and jam it hard against the exposed skin of the soldier's neck. Cody gasped, certain that Kai had just killed him.

As Cody and Taryn caught up, however, they saw that Kai had used a Taser on the soldier. He lay still on the ground, the acrid smell of burned flesh hanging in the stuffy hallway. Kai reached down and zapped him again for good measure. Then he knocked on the lab door with a precise series of raps.

Brandon pulled it open and smiled. They were in the lab.

Kai pulled the limp body of the soldier in behind them and shut the door. "Let's go," he said. "We should be out of here in three minutes."

He handed out headlamps to everyone. Cody turned her light on and began to look around the lab. She felt a surge of excitement at seeing all the beautiful science equipment. It put her high school to shame and obviously was a far cry from the antique science junk that she collected. She imagined what she could do with such perfect tools. This was somewhere she would have aspired to work one day, that future outside of Shasta where she fulfilled the promise of her lucky break and tried to pay it back. But that future didn't make sense anymore, and now she saw the gleaming microscopes and trays of beakers for what they were: tools to destroy the Ones. She turned to Brandon.

"Where's the room with the Vaccine?"

He pointed to the back of the lab, and they all walked over, with Taryn rolling the suitcase behind them. They gingerly laid it down against the door and unzipped it. The wires and tubes of the bomb sparkled under the glare of their headlamps. They were all staring at it.

Kai got on his knees and started to connect some of the wires. He turned on the cell phone that was attached to the detonator. As Kai worked, Cody stepped close to the door of the Vaccine room. She tried the doorknob—it was locked, of course—and Cody could feel how heavy the door was. This is as close as she would get. Whatever scientific miracle James's dad had figured out, she wouldn't get to see it. She hoped no one would.

"All right, she's ready," Kai said, and stood up.

They all instinctively took a step back from the bomb.

"No use hanging around—let's go," Taryn said.

They walked briskly back toward the lab entrance. The soldier on the ground was beginning to stir. Kai bent down and used the Taser on him again.

"What are we going to do with him?" Cody asked.

"Let's drag him to the stairwell. He should be protected from the blast there. Come on, give me a hand," Kai said.

They each picked up a limb and shuffled out of the lab and into the hallway. Taryn pushed open the door to the stairwell, and they dropped the soldier and proceeded down the stairs, their pace quickening. They tried to act normal as they passed the security guard in the lobby, but they were practically racing. And then, finally, they were outside, approaching the van and climbing into it, now just a phone call away from watching the beautiful explosion in their rearview mirror.

That was when Cody saw the car.

She would have recognized it anyway, but she had also just driven in it a few days earlier. It was the old-fashioned station wagon that James's father drove.

Cody watched as Arthur parked right in front of the building, turned the car off, and started walking inside.

Meanwhile, Kai was steering their van out of the parking lot and taking out a cell phone, ready to dial.

"Kai, wait! It's him! He's going inside!"

The others looked up and watched Arthur enter the

building. There was no doubt he'd be entering the lab in a matter of seconds.

"Kai, you promised me," Cody said sternly. "Don't you dare dial that number."

"Cody, he'll find the bomb. We don't have a choice," Kai said.

"I don't care. Put the phone down."

"Kai, dial the number," Taryn said.

"Shut up!" Cody shouted. "We can't kill him. We agreed."

"Cody, I'm sorry. He picked a bad time to come into work," Kai said.

"Kai, put the phone down," Cody said again.

"I didn't mean for this to happen, but he deserves it. I know he saved you, but he still created the fucking Vaccine!" Kai yelled.

"Kai, don't. Please, I beg you."

"Damn it, Kai, just do it!" Taryn shouted.

"Put the phone down, Kai, you don't have to do this!"

"Do it, already!"

Cody saw Kai lift the phone and start typing in a number, and she knew she'd never convince him. So she flung open the van doors, jumped out into the road, and started sprinting toward the science building. She had to pay her debt to James's father. She had to pay her debt to James. She couldn't let him lose his dad.

After two steps, Cody was at top speed, flying across the pavement back through the parking lot, fifty yards from the science building. She heard Kai shout after her, but she didn't turn around. She ran straight toward the doors, ran as if her life depended on it, ran as if her soul hung in the balance. She ran to save herself, and she ran to protect James. She ran to be different from Ms. Bixley and Marco and Agent Norton. She ran to thank her mother. She ran because she still knew right from wrong.

And then the explosion blasted her straight into oblivion.

CHAPTER 18

JAMES REFUSED TO speak at his father's funeral.

It was a beautiful Saturday, three days after the explosion at the laboratory, and the church was packed. His mother encouraged him to say a few words, but James couldn't do it. He knew what he was supposed to say, but he also knew it would have come out hollow and insincere. That didn't help anyone. So he told his mom that he was too crushed to give a eulogy. She understood. She didn't speak, either.

For most of the service, James stared at the shiny casket resting just in front of him. *What could possibly be in there?* he wondered. James had seen the bombing site on campus—it was basically just a smoldering crater. Even his father's car had been burned to a crisp. There were no bodies, no personal belongings. Just the certainty that his father had been inside. As James walked around the perimeter the day after the bombing, he considered what had been accomplished. The lab with the Vaccine was destroyed. He knew that was a good thing. But the one man who could save James from it, the only person who was trying to find a reasonable solution, was gone. Murdered.

And now James stared at an empty casket.

When he stood with the other pallbearers and lifted it on his shoulders, it didn't feel light. It weighed down on him just as much as if a body had been inside. As he proceeded slowly down the aisle of the church, his emotions finally overwhelmed him. He would never ride on his father's shoulders and eat ice cream again. Today, his father rode on James's shoulders.

They drove in a long procession to the cemetery outside town. It was in a sloping field at the edge of the foothills. James sat silently by the gravestone as the casket was lowered into the ground. There was a prayer. A wreath. And then the handfuls of earth that landed with a hollow thump.

It was over pretty quickly, and everyone began to file slowly back to their cars. James lingered for a bit with his mother and Michael. They had their last moment as a family, then they began to walk away, too.

James had gone only a few steps when a man in a suit gave him a friendly wave.

"It's James, right?" the man asked. He took off his dark

sunglasses and offered a handshake. James took it in a daze, as he had been doing the whole day. "I'm sorry about your father. He was a wonderful man."

"Thank you," James said, and started to walk away.

"There's something he'd probably want me to tell you," the man said.

James stopped in his tracks and turned around. "Did you work with him?" he asked, trying to hide his intense curiosity.

"A long time ago. But I kept an eye on what he was doing. We stayed in touch."

This man knew about the Vaccine, then. He seemed friendly, but James knew he should tread lightly.

"Your dad did a lot of great work for the government. You know how it is—the Department of Agriculture can never get enough corn, right?"

James nodded and forced himself to smile.

"Well, he made some arrangements with a few of his friends over there—"

"In the Department of Agriculture," James said.

"Yeah, like I said," the man in the suit continued. "Anyway, I'm sure you've seen all this hullabaloo about the new residential camps for the Ones. And I'm sure you know that the mandatory report date is tomorrow."

Of course James knew about tomorrow. Like all the other Ones in his town, he was supposed to get on a bus bound for what was sure to be some horrific concentration camp. It was all to help the country deal with the Ones in a more "organized and productive" manner, as the government had put it. James hadn't decided what he was going to do yet. Some of the older Ones had obviously made the choice to disappear already, to go live underground, maybe slip into Canada or Mexico and hopefully wait out the Equality Movement in the shadows. James, with a better idea than most about what awaited them at the camps, considered this tactic. But to do so would surely mean needing help from the New Weathermen. He clearly wasn't about to stoop to that. Submitting to the camps wasn't any better, obviously, so James was torn. There were only a few hours left to decide, but it seemed like this stranger at his father's funeral had some relevant information.

"I know what tomorrow is," he replied.

"Then you should know those friends of your father are going to honor their promise to him." The man paused. "You are not required to report to a camp. The local Equality Team has been made aware, and they won't be contacting you. The deal is contingent on keeping this between us, is that clear?"

James nodded, not relieved but shaken by this turn of events. The man looked back up to the top of the cemetery hill.

"You can thank your father," he said. "And again, my condolences."

The man walked away and left James alone among the gravestones. He couldn't believe what his father had done for him. It was a bitter irony. To be granted such a gigantic favor, his dad must have done some truly commendable work on the Vaccine. And as he had said, he'd always planned on saving James. This didn't vindicate him in James's eyes, but he was still moved that his dad was looking out for him. He almost wished he could thank him—but what was left of his dad was unrecognizable and already underground. The churning of bitterness and grief in his stomach made James feel as if he had lost his father twice in a matter of days.

James, alone in the cemetery now, was about to continue his walk down the gentle hill when a flash of movement caught his eye. He turned his head and squinted. Sure enough, there was Cody, her face concealed by a baggy hooded sweatshirt. She was across the cemetery, not exactly hiding but keeping her distance. James stopped and stared at her. He wasn't ready to see her and hadn't imagined this encounter would take place here. But now that she was in front of him, he couldn't resist. He had held his anger in all day, and he was primed to explode. God, how he needed this. He marched straight over to her.

"James," Cody started to say when he was within earshot. "I'm so sorry—"

"Shut up, I don't want to hear it," he snapped.

Cody recoiled in shock.

"You knew this was going to happen, didn't you? You knew they were going to kill him!"

"It was an accident, James, I swear."

"Why didn't you stop them? Kai is obsessed with you. He would have listened."

Cody tensed up at the word *obsessed* but recovered quickly. "The plan was to bomb the lab in the middle of the night when no one was there. To blow up *the Vaccine*. No one meant to kill your father. I made them promise!"

"Cody, he saved your life! Do you remember that? Do you know where'd you be without him?"

"James, I tried, I swear. I said I wouldn't go unless we spared him. And then I tried to save him."

James couldn't believe what he was hearing. "You were there?"

Cody didn't answer. Instead, she pulled down the hood of her sweatshirt. James couldn't help but grimace at the burn marks on her forehead, the bruises around her eyes, and the crusty bandages wrapped around her head. Her beautiful hair was burned at the ends, and she had obviously cut some off around her face. She must have been within spitting distance of the bomb when it went off. Still, despite how painful it looked, James hardened himself to her injuries. He couldn't believe that Cody had been instrumental in the death of his father.

"You put that bomb in his office, right? What did you

think would happen?" he asked. "My God, Cody, what have you become?"

James saw Cody's countenance change from compassion to anger.

"I'm the same as I ever was, James. I stand up for what's right. Your dad was creating something to destroy the Ones. I am sorry he's dead, but he shouldn't have been—"

"He was trying to help us!" James yelled. Then he remembered that Cody wasn't a One. She was in no danger of getting the Vaccine. "Trying to help the Ones, that is. He was finding a safe solution. The other people in the project wanted to lobotomize us. My dad was going to prevent that." It felt strange to suddenly be defending his father, but it was also a relief.

"At least that's what he told you."

"It's the truth! But I guess it's too late to prove it now. You murdered him. You ran off with Kai and the Weathermen, and you murdered my father."

Cody sighed. "I'm sorry you feel that way. I came here to pay my condolences, not to fight."

"Well, you shouldn't have come. You can take your condolences and stay away from my family."

"James, it doesn't have to be like this."

"Go away, Cody! You left once—do it for real this time."

James glared at her, but Cody didn't budge.

"I always meant to come back, James. I told you, I

261

needed to go somewhere terrible, and I didn't want to take you there. I thought that you'd have faith in me."

"I did." James pointed back to his father's grave. "And this is where it got me. Now go."

Cody hesitated. "The Equality Team will be in town by tomorrow. They are going to try to put all the Ones on a bus. Ship them off to a camp—you included. We're not going to let that happen to us. We've decided to stand up and fight. You should fight with us, James."

"I'm not like you. You are terrorists."

"So you'll get in line with the other sheep and march to the slaughter?" Cody asked with disgust. "Tomorrow we aren't terrorists. Tomorrow we'll just be Americans fighting for our freedom."

She was starting to sound like Kai. James didn't know who she was anymore. And he decided not to tell her what he had just learned from his father's colleague. He knew she would just throw it back in his face—the rich kid always catching a break.

"I'll be fine," he said. "I'll figure something out that doesn't involve destroying the people I love. You guys are just going to get yourselves killed."

Cody looked at the ground, clearly disappointed. "Well, then I guess this is probably the last time you'll see me." She took a deep breath and reached out to take James's hand as tears filled her eyes. "PQ3318, right?"

James didn't move, and he didn't respond.

After an excruciating moment, Cody's hand fell limply back to her side. She spoke through her tears. "It was real, James. The bond we had—the love—it was real, and I held it in the deepest part of my heart. I protected it to the last. I even survived off it. I still do."

James stared her straight in the eye. "It was nothing," he said. "I didn't even know who you were."

James turned his back and walked away through the gravestones.

＝

Later that night, James paced the length of his bedroom. Every few minutes he would refresh the news update on his computer and check in on the progress of the Ones' roundup. It was midnight on the East Coast already, and Equality Teams were fanned out across the region, starting to load the kids who had volunteered onto buses. If you checked only the mainstream news outlets, everything was proceeding peacefully, but James found plenty of first-person reports of ugly violence already breaking out and shaky videos of the agents tearing kids out of their parents' arms.

The explosion at a small university in California a few days earlier had fallen off the front page, of course. And anyway, there had been no report that the lab was home to an experimental project designed to re-engineer Ones. The official story, rather, was that a gas leak had mixed with some volatile chemistry materials and turned the building into a crater. One professor, working deep into the night, was killed. Two security guards were in the hospital.

James clicked through images from the roundup, feeling a mix of shame and relief. His family would be spared a knock on their front door tomorrow, but what had they done to earn that privilege? James could remain in his home, but what did that even mean anymore? Who was left for him here? His mother was in shock. His brother was enraged. Cody was probably going to die fighting tomorrow. And all the other Ones would disappear into the camps or go underground. If James had felt isolated before, as a member of a one-percent minority—an island in history—then he was about to get a rude awakening. After tomorrow, James would truly be alone.

As he kept pacing, there was a knock on his bedroom door. Michael cracked it open and stuck his head inside.

"Hey, how's it going?" Michael said.

"You know, not great."

Michael sat down on James's bed. He stared at the wall, obviously reeling and exhausted. "He didn't deserve it, James. He really didn't deserve it."

"I know."

"He was trying to help! These animals are so stupid; they don't even realize he was helping them."

James just nodded. Michael sat in silence for a bit, his body tense with rage. Then he turned to James.

"I saw you talking with Cody after the funeral. What was that about?"

"She knew she wasn't welcome, but she wanted to pay her respects."

"She's running around with the people who did this, right?"

"No. Not with the crazies. She would never go that far," James lied.

Michael stared at him for a moment. "Well, they deserve what's coming to them. I don't mean the camps, you know, for all the normal Ones. I'm sure that will be fine. The people who killed Dad, though . . . they deserve to burn in hell." James didn't respond, so Michael continued. "I'm going to make sure of that."

"What does that mean?" James asked.

"I'm joining one of the Equality Teams. They need local guides tomorrow, people who know the lay of the land. There are rumors of Ones hiding in the mines. They think it's that group, the New Weathermen. It's going to be like shooting fish in a barrel up there."

"Michael, what's the point? Let them handle it without you. You're not going to bring Dad back."

"The point is to punish the assholes who killed our father! I thought you might want to join me."

"Nobody deserves to die tomorrow," James said.

"But Dad did?"

James had to think about that. He saw Michael grow disgusted at his hesitation.

"Jesus, James, don't you remember what he said? He was trying to help you guys. He was the only one protecting you all from turning into zombies. Why can't you understand that?"

James didn't understand it—that was the honest truth. But he tried to convince himself again. Maybe his father's compromise was the best solution to an impossible problem. A generation was coming of age that would turn everyone else into second-class citizens. But those people still had all the power, and they weren't going to be made obsolete without a fight. Something had to give, and maybe his father had the best answer. In James's heart, that is truly what he believed. So maybe he could answer Michael's question.

"You're right. He didn't deserve to die," James said.

Michael nodded, relieved. He reached out to James and slapped him on the thigh. It was the closest thing to a hug that they could muster right now and their first physical contact since the fight. They sat like that for a while, their uncomfortable tension put aside for the moment, just two brothers mourning a father.

Michael finally stood up and moved to the door. He shook his head, a pained expression on his face. "I still don't understand how they knew, though. Dad said it was completely top secret. How could they have found out about the lab?"

James tensed up, but his brother was lost in his own world and walked out of the bedroom, still muttering to himself. James shut the door, then leaned against it and grabbed his head with both hands, trying to relieve the tremendous pressure that was building.

How did they know to bomb the lab?

James couldn't bring himself to answer that. It was too simple. The real question was more complicated: Who was truly to blame for his father's death?

James knew how he wanted to answer that question. Kai was clearly a maniac. He wanted to create chaos, sow fear, let the streets run red with the blood of his enemies—or whatever crazy way he would phrase it. It was inevitable that he would lash out in such a destructive manner, with no regard for what he was actually accomplishing or who was getting hurt. He was a zealot, and even though James agreed with his broad points, Kai had become a delusional, violent madman.

Then there was Cody. She had seen that his father was in the office after they planted the bomb. She'd had the power to stop it. And she should have known better than to indict his father without knowing all the facts. Arthur had saved her. And she watched him die.

Of course there was his dad, too: a respected professor,

a father, a man who agreed to work on a vaccine that would dismantle the identities of hundreds of thousands of people. He walked into that lab willingly every day, and the night of the bombing was no different.

Michael couldn't hide, either. He had pushed his father into this project—not overtly, but in the bitter, selfish manner that he had handled growing up with James. He had practically begged their father to find a solution to keep the peace in their family.

For that matter, maybe it was the long-deceased Thomas who set this tragedy in motion. Had he not fallen off that ledge in the quarry, James wouldn't exist. Michael wouldn't be bitter. Arthur wouldn't be desperate. The bomb wouldn't have touched them.

Yes, James concluded, they were all to blame for his father's death. They and everyone else around the country who were too stupid to handle this issue in a reasonable way. The assholes who painted equal signs. The politicians who groveled for votes. The masses of citizens who knew something immoral was taking place but refused to speak up. They didn't detonate the bomb, but they watched every step of the way as the Ones were stripped of their rights and backed into a corner. Sure, the Ones were different, and their existence was unfamiliar. But the Ones were people—kids, really—first and foremost. The accommodators, the collaborators, the silent cowards, and the naked perpetrators: They were all the same now.

That was who shouldered the blame. Kai. Cody. Arthur. Michael. Thomas. Ms. Bixley. Marco. Taryn. The whole country. Everyone who wasn't James.

Not James.

It wasn't James.

It wasn't his fault.

He didn't murder his dad.

James paced the room frantically now, saying it over and over in his own head.

It wasn't my fault.

The faster he moved, the louder he shouted in his mind.

It wasn't my fault. It wasn't my fault.

The pressure in his head was excruciating. He felt like it was about to explode.

It wasn't my fault. It wasn't my fault. It wasn't my fault.

And then James couldn't take it any longer. He let out a wail and collapsed to the floor.

He started sobbing, finally accepting the truth that he had tried so hard to deny over the past few days: He was to blame for his father's death. James, more than anyone else. He had let him walk blindly into an assassination. He had known exactly what Kai would do with the memo, and he still said nothing.

All he'd needed to do was warn him. A simple explanation that James had lost the memo to the New Weathermen and his dad would be alive right now. Maybe he'd be overseeing his version of the Vaccine at the internment camps.

Maybe he'd be saving the Ones from the more gruesome fate that awaited them.

But James hadn't said a word. He'd killed his father.

As James lay on the floor, coming to terms with this sin, his thoughts turned to Cody. He had excoriated her for the very crime that he now knew was his own. He had wanted to blame someone else so badly that he said whatever he could to support his delusion. He had been mean and abusive.

And worst of all, he had lied about loving her.

Now Cody was probably going to die tomorrow, up in the mines. He knew that was where they were, and if Michael had mentioned it, then the Equality Teams knew, too. The Weathermen versus the military was hardly a fair fight. The Ones would lose, no matter how passionately they wanted to avoid being herded into a camp. The Equality agents had guns and trucks and drones and endless reinforcements. James had watched them being used all night long on the news.

He had to see Cody again. Yes, she had run off with Kai, and she had been there at the bombing, and James's ever logical mind knew that was unforgivable. But his heart told him differently, and he couldn't stand the thought of never seeing her again, of never holding her, never laughing with her, never trailing his fingertips down the curve of her back. She was the only person who truly knew him, who appreciated him for his imperfections instead of all

the other surface-level things that made him seem perfect. And now James saw that their bond was even deeper:
Both had been prevented from forging their own identity.
Cody had been tricked, she would never know how much
perfection she could have achieved without the original
lie. And James had been sculpted as a replacement, he
would never know if that was the person he was meant to
become. But together, maybe, they could discover their
own path.

James had to see her one last time. It was all that mat-
tered to him now. Joining her fight at the mine probably
wouldn't help them beat the Equality Team, but at least
he could try. And he could apologize to her. He could
shout it to the heavens. He could admit that what she
believed was, in fact, true: Their love was real.

James's desire to reunite with Cody prompted another
desire. If he did find her, he didn't want tomorrow to be
their last day together. He didn't want only a moment
to redeem himself; he wanted a lifetime. James was spared
from going to the camps, and Cody—no longer a One—
wouldn't have to go, either. But James knew he'd never per-
suade her to abandon the other Ones.

That meant the only way to save her was to win the
fight.

James channeled his newfound energy into figuring out
how they could slay Goliath. The Equality Team would be
in Shasta by dawn. Before then, he needed to find a sling.

And just like that, midstride in a frantic race back and forth across his room, it hit him. James turned on his heel and headed straight for the garage.

=

Five hours later, James finally stopped deep in the foothills below Mount Shasta and leaned against a dry old pine tree to catch his breath. He had been at a dead run since he'd left his house, stopping only to check his map and his old Boy Scout compass by flashlight. This was his last stop: a deep, windless gully several miles north of the town. Everything else had been set up, and James had to trust in his plan now. He took off his backpack, which was much lighter now that the container of gasoline was almost empty. He poured out what was left and tossed it aside.

Then, as the first shades of dawn kissed the night sky, James knelt down and struck a match.

CHAPTER 19

THE FIRST HUMVEE rolled into the basin of the mine right after dawn. Cody watched from the edge of a small tunnel high up on the hillside, an old shotgun at her side. A line of vehicles followed along the only road that led into the mining area. It was exactly how they had planned it: The Ones had made sure that their presence in the mine wasn't a secret anymore—they knew people in town would direct the Equality Team there. Right into their trap.

The New Weathermen and several more Ones who had joined them had been busy in the four days since the announcement about the internment camps. Their plan was to make their stand in the area around the mine and the quarry. It gave them the advantages of cover, knowing the terrain, and escape routes in the tunnels. They had rigged various areas with explosives—a mishmash of rudimentary pipe bombs and Molotov cocktails—and had gathered together all the firearms they could muster.

In the best-case scenario, they could lure all the Equality agents into the basin of the mine and have snipers shoot them from concealed positions above. When the agents inevitably fought their way into the tunnels, the Ones knew which passageways were safe and which ones were rigged to collapse. Perhaps they could wipe out all the agents. Perhaps every last One would die there. What was certain, though, is that no Ones were surrendering peacefully to be dragged into a camp.

Kai made that clear when he addressed all of them in the last quiet moments before the sun came up. They had gathered in a giant cavern deep underground, and Kai waited until the only sounds were the eerie, unending reverberations of the mine.

"You hear that?" Kai asked, staring into the darkness. "Those are the echoes of every fight for freedom the world has ever known. They never die. They sink into the bones of the earth, and they hum softly, they vibrate, they rumble. And then these echoes get into *us*. They inspire us, challenge us, compel us to add our voices to their chorus." Then Kai paused, still straining to listen. "Today will be the loudest day of our lives."

He turned back to meet everyone's eyes. "A free country, right? That's always what we've been told? But the people coming here today are trying to lock us in a camp.

Trying to change the way we think. Trying to change who we are. I, for one, am not going to let that happen. But more important, no one should ever live in fear of this threat. That's the rule we live by and that's what we fight for today—the right of every person on this earth to be who they are, to live as they were born. We fight for freedom! And when we fight for freedom, we can't lose. We either win the day or we become echoes."

Kai's eyes finally landed on Cody, and she held his gaze, chills running down her spine. Whichever path the day took, she was ready to join him.

As all the Ones rushed to their assigned posts, Cody ran through her mental checklist of what she was supposed to do. Unlike everyone else, she had heard the plan only the day before. For the two days prior, while the Ones had worked to set up their defense of the mine, Cody had been unconscious.

The blast from the bomb had thrown her backward thirty feet through the air. This was according to Kai and Taryn, who scooped her limp body off the pavement, threw her into the van, and sped away from the campus. Cody didn't remember much from that night. They said her clothes were on fire, but Cody had basically survived in one piece. She woke up in the mine two days later with a horrible headache, sore all over, and with bits of gravel still embedded wherever she'd had exposed skin. It was obvious to her as she gathered her senses that she hadn't stopped the bombing. And she hadn't saved James's father.

That was why the first thing she did was find James at the cemetery. Of course, that hadn't gone exactly as planned, and now Cody was recovering from that second detonation: James didn't want to see her again. He claimed he never loved her. It was a bitter moment that very well might be their last.

Cody was devastated by what James said, and she took her anger out on Kai after she made it back to the mine yesterday.

"Some promise, huh?" she said with a withering look.

"I'm sorry he died, Cody. And I'm sorry you got hurt. But I did what I had to do."

"So your word means nothing, then?"

"My word isn't more important than our fight. The lab is gone now. We don't have to talk about it, but I know you agree with what I did," Kai said.

Cody looked at him with disgust. "You think I agree with what happened that night?"

"If you didn't, you wouldn't have come back here."

Kai said it softly, not to score a point but to let her know he understood. Even as Cody fumed, she knew he was right. And even more infuriating, she liked him more for standing up to her about it.

Despite her anger over being deceived, Cody did agree with him, and she had spent the rest of day coming to terms with that. The Equality Team was on its way, and Cody needed to prepare herself. The people who had imprisoned and tortured her were coming for all the Ones now. Innocent people were about to be forced into camps and vaccinated. Cody had to do everything she could to stop this. It may have seemed like a decision that Cody had made when she was released from her detention, but the truth was that she had always been ready to take this stand. From the moment she first saw someone being persecuted for how they were born, Cody was unwavering. She would fight against it until her last breath. She would join Kai in becoming an echo.

As Cody considered the events of the past day, the moment finally arrived. Down below her in the mine, the silence of the clear, beautiful morning was broken by the crackle of a bullhorn set atop one of the Equality vehicles.

"By order of the United States Congress, you are lawfully required to report to your assigned camps. This is your last opportunity to do so peacefully. If you do not, we will take you into custody by force."

The screech of the bullhorn echoed off the limestone walls, and the mine was quiet again. After a few moments, the Humvees disgorged two dozen Equality agents—all armed to the teeth—plus a few civilians decked out in hunting gear. They began to scan the walls of the mine and inch forward.

Cody hefted the shotgun into her hands. Its weight was surprisingly comforting. She had been practicing only a day or so, shooting at tree branches, but she was an adequate shot. Ready to fire, she scanned the other tunnels where she knew the Ones were hiding. Brandon had his eye pressed against a rifle sight, perfectly prepared. Daphne knelt calmly, looking like her heart rate had barely changed. J-Dog stared down at the agents intently, his hair spiked in a wild mane and his nostrils flaring with every breath. When the moment was right, they would all try to shoot as many agents as they could. But from this distance and with the old rifles and pistols they had scrounged up, she wasn't sure if their fire would actually hit anyone. Instead, it would hopefully draw the Equality Team into the mining tunnels.

Bam!

Cody jumped as the first shot rang out from above her. She saw dust kick up near a Humvee, and then all the agents were facing her direction, unleashing a volley of rifle fire. Cody ducked back into her tunnel, not even firing a shot. She heard other guns firing from around the mine, but they sounded pitiful next to the loud automatic weapons of the Equality Team. The hot, acrid smell of gunpowder quickly drifted into her cavern. Crawling back to the edge of her tunnel, she looked down into the basin. The Humvees had been driven into a tight circle, and now the agents stood in the center, shooting up from their covered position. Shots continued to ring out from the Ones, but they clearly weren't effective. The two sides were at an impasse. Cody knew that was fine for the Ones. They had stockpiled food and water for days, and they knew the Equality Team wanted no part in a drawn-out siege. The Ones were supposed to all be in the camps by the end of the day. If a few kids hiding in the woods managed to hold out, it would be a national embarrassment.

Cody decided to leave her position and check in with Kai. She backtracked through the tunnels and found her way to Kai's perch.

"What do you think?" she asked as she knelt next to him.

"We're fine. We keep taking these potshots at them, and they'll be forced to come after us. Once we start popping the tunnels, you know where to go, right?"

Cody nodded and pulled up her shirtsleeve. An intricate map of lines was drawn in pen and snaked all the way up her arm.

Kai smiled. "Great. Now just don't break a sweat." Then he saw something below. "What are they doing?"

Cody peered out also and saw an Equality agent loading a grenade launcher on his shoulder. He aimed at the slope of the mine and fired into the farthest-left tunnel. There was a burst of flames, dust erupted into the air, and then the tunnel was gone, collapsed into the hillside. The agent rotated a little and fired at the next tunnel on the left. This time he hit a location that the Ones had rigged to blow. The explosion was massive, and now this tunnel suddenly disappeared, too. Cody knew someone was in there. That person was dead now.

Kai looked on in horror. "They're not going to set foot in these tunnels . . ."

And as Cody watched a third grenade get launched, this one shaking the walls around her, she realized it, too. "They don't care about capturing us. They're happy to bury us alive."

It was the first time Cody had ever seen Kai look scared. His hair had grown in a little more, and it made him look younger—more his actual age. He was still a young man, too. And he was probably going to die today.

Kai leaned outside, exposing himself but trying to get an angle to shoot the agent firing the grenade launcher. It was impossible, though: The agent was too protected by the Humvees. Cody saw that their plans were now falling apart. If the Equality Team was willing to patiently destroy the entrance to every tunnel instead of coming after them, all their traps were useless.

"Come on," she said, grabbing Kai's shoulder. "We have to get out of here before all the exits collapse."

Kai pushed her away. "We can't beat them in the open. We have to hold the mine."

"Kai, the mine is a death trap now! They are going to level it."

Several other Ones had joined them in the tunnel. Every few seconds, explosions rang out around them, each one getting closer and shaking dust onto their heads.

"Fine!" Kai shouted. "Let's get out through the back and then fan out on the ridge above the mine. Maybe we can keep them pinned in the basin from there."

Kai grabbed his rifle and started jogging deeper into the mine. Cody and the other Ones followed. After a few minutes of switching tunnels and climbing upward, they emerged in the woods near the top of the mine. Cody was grateful that she hadn't been forced to escape on her own—the map on her arm was now an ink splotch streaked with sweat.

The Ones rushed back to the area above the mine and spread out through the trees that edged up to the cliffs. Below them, the Equality Team was still firing grenades into the tunnels. When the Ones shot from above, they'd draw the attention of the agents, but they had no choice. The first plan had backfired, and this was as good a defensive position as they could hope for now. It was fight here or run.

Cody hunkered down next to Kai and Taryn, and they began firing down at the Humvees. The agents reacted, half of them firing back and the others jumping into the vehicles and driving out of the basin. Cody followed the curve of the mining road and saw that they would soon be attacked from the side, as well. Still, they held their position and kept shooting into the belly of the mine.

As they fought, Cody got her first whiff of the smoke.

The wind began to bring a powerful scent of scorched wood, and she looked up to the horizon and froze. Coming toward them from the east, in front of the rising sun, a gigantic cloud of black smoke had started to conceal the sky. It was beautiful and terrifying all at once, and Cody was so transfixed that she lowered her gun. Kai looked over to see why she had stopped shooting and saw for himself.

"Holy shit," he said. He nudged Taryn to look, and the three of them stared at the horizon as a wall of flames marched toward them.

The entire forest was on fire.

Even from a great distance, they could already feel the heat. Thick smoke drifted over them now. And a faint roar grew ever louder—the sound of the fire crackling everything in its path.

At that moment, the Equality Team that had driven up to outflank them started shooting from the side. The Ones were now being fired upon from two directions, and the agents who had reached the top of the cliff were advancing easily. A bullet struck the rock next to Cody's head, pelting her with shards of stone. She ducked down and fired back, but it was clear that their fight was almost over. Cody started to accept that she might die on this ridge. She certainly wasn't going to surrender.

Cody shared a look with Kai and knew he was thinking the same thing. He nodded to her gravely but with admiration in his eyes. The enemy they opposed was formidable, but they hadn't backed down. They had fought to protect the rights and the lives of the Ones. They had fought for freedom. If this was how that fight ended, they could die with pride.

"I wish I could have shown you the Ark one day," Kai said. "I think you would have really liked it. And I think you would have liked Edith Vale."

What did he just say? Cody jerked her head toward him. "Edith Vale? The Ark? Kai, tell me what you're talking about!"

A volley of bullets whistled past their ears, and they dove to the ground. All Cody wanted now was to hear Kai explain himself, but he simply held her gaze, reached out to take her hand, and squeezed it. Cody felt the charge in his fingertips and realized that this was all she'd ever share with him. It wasn't enough, she thought. Kai's mysteries were infinite, and she suddenly felt desperate to unravel them.

Wishing couldn't save them, though, so Cody lay shoulder to shoulder with Kai and Taryn, firing their last bullets at the advancing Equality Team. As they emptied their guns, Cody heard someone step on a branch directly behind them. All three wheeled around, ready to charge and fight with tooth and nail.

But standing in front of them was James.

"If you follow me right now, I can get you out of here," he said.

Cody was too startled to answer. She couldn't believe he had joined them. And she really wanted to slap him across the face.

"We're not running from this fight," Kai said. He turned to Cody and Taryn. "We promised we wouldn't run. They'll just chase us down and take us away."

"No, they won't," James said.

Cody heard the authority in his voice, and a glimmer of hope grew inside of her. "What do you mean?" she asked.

"I started the fire," he said, which Cody now realized should have been obvious, considering his haggard look, the soot all over his face, and the ax hooked into his belt. "I set it up so there's only one way out of this valley. If we go right now, we can still make it."

Gunshots rang out above their heads, and they all ducked down together.

Kai looked into the distance at the fire approaching from the east. "Set it up?" he scoffed. "That's a forest fire—we have no idea how it will move! We can't run toward it and expect to live. We might as well stay and fight."

"I know exactly how it will move. I started a blaze on the valley floor that's moving toward us on the easterly winds. And I just set another blaze higher up on Mount Shasta. It's going to travel west, following the slope of the hill. Picture elevator doors that meet in the middle," James said, and demonstrated by slowly pushing his palms together. "We don't want to be here when they close."

Cody craned her neck to look to the west. Sure enough, she saw the first wisps of smoke drifting up from the trees on Mount Shasta. James had placed them in a vise that was slowly getting tighter. But she had faith he could get them out of it. And she almost smiled—leave it to James to finally know which way the wind was blowing.

"Great, a wall of wildfire coming from both directions," Taryn said. "The river cuts us off to the north, and the Equality assholes are blocking us from the town. I hope you brought some marshmallows."

"We can cross the river."

"There are only rapids up here. We'll get crushed," Kai said.

James turned and set his gaze solely on Kai for the first time. Cody saw the fury building in his eyes. He grabbed Kai by the collar and in one powerful motion slammed his back against the rock they were hiding behind.

"Then stay here and burn, for all I care!" James said through clenched teeth.

Kai and James held their position, faces almost touching,

bodies tense. And then Kai put his hands up and gave an almost imperceptible nod of submission. Cody knew it wasn't over between these two, but now wasn't the time.

"James, he's right about the rapids. What are we going to do at the river?" Cody said, trying to get them back on track.

"There's one spot we can cross. If you follow me, I'll get us out. But I'm leaving right now," James said.

And then Cody saw him stare only at her. He didn't speak for a moment, even as the bullets and the smoke and the roar of the flames threatened to overwhelm them. "I'm sorry, Cody. I always knew exactly who you were. And I *did* love you. I still do."

Cody stared right back into his eyes. Her heart burst open, and a tiny smile snuck onto her face. "Then we better start running."

James pivoted instantly and took off into the trees, his backpack and ax bouncing with every stride. Cody followed right behind, and she could feel Kai and Taryn join them. Unfortunately, there was no time and no way to alert their comrades. It was just the four of them now—running at a dead sprint, ducking bullets and winding through the thickening smoke. James set a torrid pace, but Cody had no trouble staying right with him. Kai and Taryn were game to keep up, and the four teenagers crashed through the woods like a landslide. The only thing louder than their relentless stomping was the roar of the fire next to them.

The blaze from the east had rushed up the slope of the valley, and now sparks and ashes rained down on them. Cody saw James veer to the west a little, but that was hardly any better. She could already hear the wall of wildfire rolling down Mount Shasta. The safe passage of their corridor was narrowing by the second on both sides.

They ran harder still, leaping over logs, scrambling over rocks, and bouncing off the sturdy pine trees. As they crossed an open meadow, gunshots rang out from behind them. The Equality Team had kept up their pursuit and drawn near. Forced to go faster, Cody felt her lungs start to burn from the smoke and her eyes begin to tear. It was hard to keep sight of James through the haze, but she followed the sounds of his crashing footsteps. Sweat poured off her now, and she felt as if her body were being baked from the inside. But she knew how to run when her body begged her not to. She turned her brain off, kept her legs churning, and found her final gear. Just a normal run through the woods.

At last, Cody heard something other than the roar of the fire. She made out the sounds of the rapids; the rush of the river was just ahead of them. *Come hell or high water*, Cody thought. They'd really decided to prove the old saying—and also added some sadistic federal agents to the mix.

But as they gathered on the riverbank, catching their breath, Cody felt utter defeat. The river was moving way too fast. If they tried to wade across, they would be carried away and smashed on the rocks. Cody glanced to the west and the east. The wildfires were soon going to meet on top of them.

"See! We can't cross!" Kai yelled at James.

James, too winded to speak, motioned for them to follow him down the riverbank. They jogged along the shore for a hundred yards, and then Cody saw it.

The beaver dam.

It was a well-known hiking destination, a marvel of animal ingenuity, and maybe today, a lifeline out of the fire.

The dam extended from the near bank about halfway across the river. It was built up against a giant boulder that rested in the middle of the rapids. The boulder took up another quarter of the river's width. Once they traversed the dam and the adjoining rock, the boulder might be high enough for them to leap over the surging water and land in the shallows on the far bank. They'd have to try. The other choices were fire, fire, or the Equality Team.

James led them out over the beaver dam. It was hard to find footing on the uneven piles of gnawed-down sticks. A fall would send them into the rapids, so they proceeded slowly. When they all crowded onto the boulder in the middle of the river, they peered over the side that faced the far bank. A running leap would be enough to land in a safe area. And best of all, the fire hadn't jumped the river. It looked like Eden over there.

As they prepared to leap, Cody saw the Equality Team emerge from the woods at the same spot a few hundred yards up the river. She pointed them out to everyone else.

"Let's go—they'll be here in a minute."

Taryn stared at the agents, an angry look falling over her face. She turned to James. "Not to be a buzzkill, but aren't they just going to follow us over the dam?"

James smiled at her. "Only if they want to get roasted," he said, then knelt down and ripped open his backpack. He took out a can of lighter fluid and a matchbook, and Cody smiled, too. He was going to burn down the only way out behind them.

For the first time all day, Cody felt like she was going to survive. They had escaped the fire. They had one more jump to clear the river. And the Equality Team would be stranded on the other side, forced to backtrack as quickly as possible toward Shasta or die in the inferno. Waves of joy flooded Cody's brain. She had been willing to die, but she wanted to live. The Ones' fight wasn't over. Agent Norton still breathed free air. And the boy she loved had saved her life again. This time she wouldn't push him away.

James went to work at the point where the dam met the boulder in the middle of the river. He doused the wood with lighter fluid and threw a match on. A few sticks caught the flame, but the fire didn't spread back across the dam to the first bank. James shook out more fluid, but the flames stubbornly wouldn't move.

Then Cody saw James look up at the sky as pure horror spread across his face. The winds had shifted.

Cody had felt it, too, but she didn't realize the magnitude of the change. There had been a strong easterly wind all morning, and if only that had persisted, James could easily burn the dam back to the shore by setting the fire from this side. Not anymore. He started walking toward their original riverbank.

"I have to set it from that side," he shouted, already moving.

"James, wait!" she yelled.

But he rushed back to the bank, shaking out more lighter fluid, even as the Equality Team was racing toward him. Kai grabbed Cody and pulled her to the edge of the boulder.

"Cody, we have to jump!"

Taryn took a running start, leaped, and made it across.

"Now you go!" Kai yelled.

"We have to wait for James!"

Cody looked on as James tried to start a fire on the far side of the dam. But instead of standing on the dam so he could backtrack toward the boulder ahead of the flames, James was kneeling on the shore. He was going to be on the wrong side of the burning dam.

"James—" she began to shout so she could correct him, but then she saw why he was positioned that way. He got the fire started, and immediately the wind propelled the flames straight across the butane-soaked dam toward the boulder. The whole structure was on fire now, and anyone who had been standing on it would have been burned immediately.

"Cody, come on, jump!" Kai yelled. He shook her as hard as he could, but she didn't move.

Cody stood motionless, staring at James. He stood on the side of the river staring back at her. The dam burned in between them, crumbling into the water. "Go," she saw him say as he held his hands up to his heart.

Then Kai grabbed her arm, started running, and pulled her with him into the air over the river. They landed with a vicious thud and a splash but managed to scramble out of the rapids. Cody tried to turn around, but Kai pulled her up into the tree line. With enough cover to avoid getting shot, Cody finally looked back for James.

The Equality agents were almost on top of him, and James had knelt down and raised his arms in surrender. The agents surrounded him, guns pointed at his head. Cody covered her mouth in horror when she recognized one of the civilians who had pursued them alongside the Equality Team.

It was Michael.

She saw James's face when he looked up and found his

brother pointing a gun at him. It was a picture of total devastation, and her heart broke for him.

Then James turned to search for Cody across the river. Amid the chaos of the roaring fire, the swirling smoke, the falling ash, the raging rapids, and the shouting agents, their eyes met for one final moment. They were far away, and only had a second to communicate before someone pulled a bag over his head, but Cody stared deep into his eyes and knew that James understood.

No matter where they take you, I will find you. No matter what it costs, I will save you. No matter how they change you, you will always be my one.

ACKNOWLEDGMENTS

I can't thank some people enough for the ways in which they contributed to this book. So I will start here and try to put a dent in my enormous debt of gratitude.

Lifelong thanks to:

Jonathan Berry, for being the first person who had the crazy idea that this could be a book. Pretty essential! And Richard Abate, half man, half wizard, half agent, for taking a leap of faith and sticking his neck out for me.

Erin Stein, my patient and savvy editor, for making this book much better, often in spite of my cluelessness. And to everyone else at Imprint and Macmillan, for busting their humps to make this book real.

Caitlin Gamble and Danny Nussbaum, for explaining a lot of science that I tried my best not to mangle.

My sister, Little E, for setting the standard with your

work ethic and moral compass, which I aimed for every day while writing.

DK, the yang to my yang, for granting me the joy of finding a One.

And lastly, to several decades' worth of teachers and professors whose gifts of inspiration, wisdom, and support I lean on every day of my life: Nancy Schustek, Mark Greenwald, Jeremy Rosenholtz, Barbara Ellis, Bob Montera, Joe Algrant, Elizabeth Bobrick, Richard Slotkin, Kit & Joe Reed, Mark Dickerman, Charlie Rubin, and George Malko.